Blood & Scripture

Memoirs of the Philadelphia Slasher

David L. Powell III

ISBN: 979-8-218-66192-2

DEDICATION

For the ones who were never heard,
whose stories ended in silence.
For the children who had to grow up too fast,
and the adults still carrying those broken pieces.

To my children—
your light keeps me grounded.
You are the only chapters I never want to rewrite.

And to the city that raised me in both chaos and
clarity—
this is for the shadows you forgot,
and the truth buried beneath your bricks.

—David L. Powell III

PREFACE

Am I a monster or salvation? The line between them is thinner than most would believe. Yet, whichever I am, the path is mine alone. I called myself salvation. Like a dark prophet, I walk this twisted path with eyes wide open, the blood of the fallen painting my hands. I do not hide from what I am, nor do I seek forgiveness. My pen bleeds the truth of my own making—a gospel carved from the sins of others and my own shattered innocence.

I've heard the whisperings, the speculations of those who believe they can unravel me with their clinical eyes and academic theories. They dissect my actions, hoping to find some sense in the madness. But they will never understand. Not truly. For them, it is an exercise in curiosity. For me, it is purpose.

I was not always what I am. There was a time when the world held fragments of beauty, when innocence was not a distant echo, but something I believed could be mine. But innocence was a lie, a fragile thing meant to be broken.

The darkness has been with me for so long now. It is both my tormentor and my sanctuary. And like any good disciple, I have learned to embrace it. I offer this confession not for forgiveness, but for understanding. To speak the truth of my deeds, to expose the ugliness that has become my only form of purity.

The heroin epidemic came first, creeping into our neighborhoods like a slow, sick tide. Needles littered the gutters, veins collapsing under the weight of desperation. But then came crack, hitting us like a plague. A poison unleashed upon our streets, devouring our youth, breaking our families. I watched mothers sell their dignity for a rock the size of a fingernail. I saw men once filled with strength and pride rot away in alleyways, their souls crumbling like ash.

Philadelphia became a battlefield, and the bodies piled higher with each passing year. They preached reform and offered hollow words, but nothing changed. The rot only spread.

And while the city crumbled, the righteous did nothing. The churches locked their doors, their prayers whispered from behind stained glass while the streets bled. They preached forgiveness and mercy, but they refused to act. Their sermons were like rain against stone.

They tell me that vengeance belongs to the Lord. That His justice is righteous and pure. But where was His justice when the poison spread through our veins? Where was His mercy when children lay dying in gutters, their bodies corrupted by addiction and despair?

They tell me that it is not my place to judge. That judgment belongs only to Him. But the Bible itself tells me otherwise. It speaks of righteousness, of purging away impurity. Of standing against the wicked when no one else will.

Proverbs 21:15 — "When justice is done, it brings joy to the righteous, but terror to evildoers."

The words burned themselves into my mind, a scripture my grandfather had once preached during Sunday service. It was something my mother would repeat, her voice slurred and broken, but the words remained whole. Even in her haze, they clung to her lips like prayers twisted into pleas. Yet even he couldn't see the truth within them. Justice is not a prayer whispered from a pulpit. It is an act. A blade drawn against the darkness.

Isaiah 1:25 — "I will turn my hand against you; I will thoroughly purge away your dross and remove all your impurities."

I am not disobeying His will. I am fulfilling it. The world has grown complacent, turning its eyes away from the poison that has consumed us. But I will not be blinded by their false mercy. I will be the hand that turns against the wicked. I will be the purifier, cutting away the infected flesh before it can spread further.

This is my testament. My confession. My truth.

You will never understand why I do what I do. But you will see it. Through these pages, you will see the truth. The truth is, I am the only one left who cares.

They speak of hope, of rebuilding what was lost. They preach of redemption from podiums and pulpits, distant and untouched by the reality festering in the streets. They have not walked among the poisoned and the damned. They have not seen the rot firsthand. They do not understand the language of blood.

I have spent years sharpening my purpose, refining the clarity of my calling. It is not hate that drives me, but love. Love for a people lost and wandering, drowned by the very filth they once swore to rise above. I have watched the strong fall and the weak devour their remains. I have witnessed men with voices like thunder reduced to mumbles and whispers beneath the weight of addiction and corruption.

Where are the saviors they were promised? Where are the guardians who swore to protect them? Where is the justice for the fallen and the forgotten?

Psalm 94:16 asks, "Who will rise up for me against the wicked? Who will take a stand for me against evildoers?"

No one else has answered that call. No one but me. I am the answer. The shepherd who leads them from darkness. The blade that cuts away the decay. The inferno that purges the world of its filth. This is my gift to you.

My confession. My testimony.

Let the world call me what it will. Let them paint me as a villain and strike my name from the records of time. I care not for their judgment.

For I have already rendered mine. And it is absolute.

THOU SHALT NOT FORGET BETRAYAL

The verse that has always stuck with me is
Proverbs 22:6. I used to whisper it to myself like a
prayer, not because I believed it would save me,
but because I wanted to believe it could. Train up
a child in the way he should go, and when he is
old he will not depart from it. But what if the path
is poison? What if the hands meant to guide you
are the ones that wound you most?

My mother read me that scripture once. I still
remember the way the words fumbled from her
lips, heavy and clumsy, like she was trying to
hold on to their weight but kept dropping pieces.
Her voice was thick—syrupy, like she'd

swallowed a bottle of molasses whole. She was high when she did it.

I don't think she even knew I was listening. Her eyes drifted from me to some invisible point on the wall where shadows from the blinds splintered and swayed. I remember that gaze—how it floated, unfocused, slipping through the cracks of reality like it was searching for something I couldn't see. I was five then, maybe six. Old enough to recognize the slur in her speech, too young to understand its source. Addiction wasn't a word I knew back then. It was just the smell of burnt spoons and the way her hands shook when she held me.

I clung to that verse like a splintered promise, whispering it to myself in the dark corners of rotting apartments and cluttered living rooms. Train up a child in the way he should go… I wanted to believe that somehow, despite the way her world spun and collapsed, she was still leading me somewhere. That I wouldn't stray. That I wouldn't forget. Even when her eyes glazed over and her fingers trembled, I held on. Because holding on felt like a lifeline—like proof that there was still a path, even if we couldn't see it anymore.

But the truth is, we never had a path—just a series of dead ends strung together by false hope and desperate deals. We drifted from place to place, hovering at the borders of neighborhoods like ghosts waiting for someone to remember us. We lived in the Richard Allen projects— apartments where the air clung heavy with desperation's residue. Curtains hung limp like forgotten dreams. The walls whispered of things done in the dark, where the sound of glass breaking, or a woman's sobs felt like a language of their own. I learned to listen to those whispers, to pick apart the stories caught in the plaster and brick.

Stains were part of the decor—brown smears from hands pressed too hard, crimson streaks that memory preferred to blur. The carpets bore the scent of mildew and spilled liquor, fibers crushed under the weight of countless failures.

Sometimes, I'd find needles tucked between cushions like secrets meant to be kept. I would hold them in my hands and wonder what kind of magic they held, what kind of escape they promised. For a long time, I thought they were hers—gifts from men who came and went, their faces hidden behind clouds of smoke and anguish.

Mom was always chasing something—a dealer with a promise wrapped in poison, a hit that would make everything right. "Baby, it's gonna be different this time," she'd whisper, her voice fevered, her fingers trembling against my scalp. Her touch was soft, almost tender, like she was brushing dust off something fragile. It was the kind of touch that should've made me feel safe, but it only left me colder. I wanted to believe her—I did. I wanted to believe that one day, she'd wake up and things would be different. But it was never different.

Every promise crumbled to dust. Her eyes would glaze over, her focus lost to the sharp point of a needle. I would watch her go under, her body sagging into the cushions like she was melting into them. And I would wait—wait for her to return from wherever she went when the world slipped away. Hunger gnawed at my ribs like a familiar ache, but I'd learned to ignore it. Hunger was patient. It knew how to wait.

There was a time when she still had light in her eyes. When her smile felt real—not the ghost of a grin but something that reached all the way to her soul. I remember it like it was yesterday—the lights, the smell of funnel cake, her laughter. We'd gone to the carnival. It must have been a good day, one of the rare ones when she managed to pull herself from the haze long enough to remember I was there. She held my hand so tightly I thought she'd never let go. I didn't want her to.

The lights flickered against the darkening sky, colors bleeding into one another as the rides spun and the music played. She laughed—really laughed—and I saw her, the real her, the one she used to be. For a moment, I let myself believe that maybe she could stay like that. Maybe the ride would stop and we'd just keep circling the lights, her hand in mine. But I knew better. Even then, I knew that good days were flukes—little stumbles of light that found their way into our shadows. I held her hand tighter, squeezing until my fingers ached, as if my grip alone could keep her in that moment. But time doesn't listen to prayers. It just keeps moving. It was the last time I saw her smile like that.

If I could have stopped the clock right there, frozen her smile in place, maybe everything would have been different. Maybe the poison wouldn't have sunk so deep. Maybe she would have kept that light in her eyes. But time, like the carousel, never stops. It just keeps turning, carrying you round and round, back to the same broken promises and empty bottles. Back to the stains that never wash out and the whispers that never fade.

Mentally I had already departed. I had been led astray before. I even knew what the path was supposed to look like. I think I always knew. Maybe that's why I held her hand so tight. Maybe that's why I whispered that verse, not because I believed it would save me, but because I was terrified it never would.

The carousel still turned in my mind, its painted horses moving up and down, round and round, even when I closed my eyes. It was endless, spinning forever in the same tight circle, just like her promises. I'd watch those horses, their frozen smiles and glassy eyes, and wonder if they knew they were trapped. If they knew that no matter how much they moved, they'd never go anywhere. Sometimes, I'd imagine her on one of those horses, waving like she did that day, only this time she never got off. Just spinning. Forever.

The carnival… it felt like magic.

The smells of funnel cake and cotton candy drifted through the air, momentarily drowning out the ever-present scent of cigarette smoke that clung to her coat.

"Look, Mama!" I exclaimed, pointing to a booth where neon-colored fish swam lazily in tiny glass bowls. She smiled—a real smile, one that reached her eyes, smoothing the hard lines of fatigue from her face. It was a smile I hadn't seen in a long time, and it filled my chest with something warm and unexplainable.

"For once," she said, her voice soft and unhurried, "we're gonna have some real fun."

We wandered from stall to stall, playing games I knew she couldn't afford but she played anyway, her laughter ringing out when I won a plastic soldier figurine. She even bought me cotton candy, its pink wisps dissolving on my tongue like dreams.

I rode the carousel so many times that day, I held on to the painted horse, gripping its mane as it bobbed up and down, the world blurring into streaks of color. She stood by the gate, waving at me, her eyes brighter than I could ever remember. It was like the darkness had been peeled away, just for this moment.

But when the ride ended, and we stepped back into the chilled night air, her smile faded. Her eyes grew distant, clouded by whatever ghosts followed her. The carnival lights didn't seem as bright anymore, and the air grew heavy with that familiar weight. I looked back at the carousel, its painted horses still moving up and down, trapped in their eternal circle.

It was the last time I saw her smile like that.

The lights of the carnival faded into memory, replaced by the sharp tang of cigarette smoke and the dull hiss of the radiator.

The magic slipped away, leaving only the heavy weight of stillness. She sat there motionless, like one of those painted horses once vibrant, full of color, now just another piece of the endless cycle, moving but going nowhere. Round and round. Nowhere to go. Just like her promises—beautiful on the surface but empty underneath... Maybe that's where the numbness began—when I stopped waiting for things to change.

There were other moments—small pockets of stillness—that I held onto. Weekends with my grandparents. Sundays meant church. Clean clothes, ironed stiff by my grandmother's hands, the smell of her lavender water lingering on the collar of my shirt. Everything smelled clean there—like a different world from the one I knew. A world untouched by smoke and shadows. She'd smooth my hair with a practiced hand, her eyes sharp and unyielding as she inspected my appearance. "The Lord sees everything, Derrick. We don't give Him less than our best," she'd say.

I'd sit between her and Grandpa in the pew, my feet not quite touching the floor, my hands clasped in my lap. The church was old—stained glass windows that cast fractured rainbows onto the wooden floors, the smell of cedar and dust mixing with the faint sweetness of incense. I never wanted it to end. In that hour, I could pretend the world was clean. Holy. Like maybe there was a place where shadows couldn't reach. I'd listen to the choir, their voices rising like smoke, filling the room with something that almost felt like hope.

Grandpa would nod along with the preacher, his Bible worn and creased, pages marked with tiny scribbles. He'd hold it open on his lap, one hand resting on its cover like it was something holy. Sometimes, he'd lean down and whisper a verse in my ear, his voice low and steady. 'The Lord is my shepherd; I shall not want.'

I didn't understand the words then. But I held on to them. Maybe because they were steady. Maybe because, for that hour, everything felt clean. Holy. Like the darkness couldn't touch us there.

But Sunday never lasted. Monday always came, dragging me back to the world I knew — the one where shadows crept in broad daylight and desperation lived in every crack of the pavement. The one where I learned not to look too closely, not to listen too hard. Survival had its own set of rules.

It was in those days that I started seeing things. Things no child should have to see. Men with knuckles tattooed by violence and veins that ran with poison. Women who traded flesh to keep the cold away. And once, a man who reduced his lover's voice to fractured breaths in the hallway of a tenement where the air hung thick with stale sweat and the sharp tang of old paint. Footsteps echoed down the hall, each one like a slow countdown. My fingers dug into the peeling wallpaper, grit settling under my nails as I held my breath, waiting for it to stop.

Men whose knuckles bore the stains of violence and veins laced with desperation. Women who bartered their bodies to chase away the chill.

I remember the first time I saw someone disappear. Not in the way that magicians do it, with curtains and applause, but in the way a shadow gets swallowed by darkness—sudden, absolute. It was in the hallway of a tenement where the air hung thick with the sour musk of decay, where desperation clung to the walls like mold and footsteps echoed like threats. The kind of place where secrets lived in the cracks of plaster and promises crumbled like dust.

I watched as he reduced her voice to fractured breaths. He shouted words I couldn't understand, his voice booming off the cracked walls like thunder. I closed my eyes and whispered it under my breath, the only verse I knew: 'The Lord is my shepherd; I shall not want.' But the walls didn't listen. My whispers couldn't drown out the sound of her sobs, the muffled thud of fists against flesh. The scripture felt hollow, just words hanging in the damp air, weightless and useless. It didn't stop the screaming. It didn't stop anything.

She was thin, jittery, her movements sharp and frantic, like a bird with broken wings. She tried to pull away, but he dragged her down with a force that bent her like brittle glass. I watched, rooted in place, my own breath tight and shallow, hands curled into fists until they throbbed. I wanted to scream, to do something, but fear sat heavy on my chest, thick and suffocating. I knew that fear. It was older than me, something passed down like a family heirloom—silent, binding, unbreakable.

But beneath that fear, something else flickered. A small, shameful whisper that I didn't want to hear. I wanted to understand what it felt like to have that kind of power—to make someone disappear, if only for a moment. To bend the world to my will, just once, and feel it yield beneath my hand. It scared me how natural that thought felt—like it had been waiting there all along, dormant but hungry.

When he left, she remained crumpled and broken, her breath threading through the silence like something half-forgotten. I watched her chest rise and fall, the struggle of it, the way life clawed its way back to her. It almost looked like hope, but I knew better. Hope didn't live in places like that. It shriveled up, curled back into itself, and died long before it ever had a chance to grow. I waited for her to scream, to sob, to do something that would let me know she was still human. But she just lay there, eyes fixed on nothing, breath thin and ragged like she was afraid to draw in too much air. I think that was the first time I wondered if death could be a kindness.

I didn't move. I stayed long enough to see her crumble, long enough to hear her voice fade into nothing, then I slipped back into the shadows, invisible again. The verse still hung in my mouth like smoke, but I didn't say it. I wasn't sure I believed it anymore. Maybe that was when I learned that trying to help only invited more pain. That the world didn't reward heroes in places like that.

When I finally stepped back, it wasn't with fear— it was with something worse. It was with nothing at all. It felt like armor, heavy but protective, numbing me to the sharpness of things I couldn't change. I think that was the first time I realized that nothingness could be a kind of power. A way to survive.

Because I had watched. Because I had survived. Because I had been untouched by the violence that consumed her. I remember thinking that power wasn't always about strength. Sometimes it was just about standing still and watching someone else disappear.

Violence wasn't always loud. Sometimes, it was quiet—whispered in the flick of a lighter or the slow melt of powder in a spoon. My mother was no stranger to it. But hers wasn't the kind that left bruises on skin. It was the kind that hollowed you out from the inside, slow and methodical, until there was nothing left to break.

I knew the steps by heart. The ritual played out like clockwork, every movement precise, practiced. Her hands would tremble, shaking like leaves caught in a bitter wind, but she never faltered. The lighter would spark, its tiny flame dancing beneath the spoon. I used to watch her eyes then—how they flickered with something like devotion. It was almost reverent, the way she handled it. Like prayer. Her lips would move sometimes, whispering to herself or to something I couldn't see. The syringe never strayed far from her reach, always within arm's length, like it was a part of her. I never knew a person could love something that much.

When the needle sank into her vein, it was like she was letting go of something heavy. Her eyes would flutter, and for a moment, I would see peace on her face—the kind of peace that only ever came with poison. I wondered sometimes if that's what she was chasing. Not the high, but the silence that came with it. The way the world went still for her, like the carousel finally stopped spinning. Maybe that's why she did it—because everything stopped hurting, even just for a little while.

Her highs were mercurial things—sometimes she'd collapse into herself, sagging into the cushions like her bones had turned to water. I'd sit there and watch her breathing, shallow and slow, wondering if this was the time she wouldn't wake up. Other times, she'd pace the apartment like a caged animal, her footsteps heavy and restless, her laughter brittle and edged with something sharp. She'd talk to people that weren't there, argue with shadows I couldn't see. I learned to stop asking who she was talking to. I learned not to listen.

But it was the stillness that frightened me most. When the high dragged her too deep, leaving her limp and dull, eyes half-lidded and breath whispering out of her like it might stop at any second. I would shake her sometimes, call her name, my voice cracking from the strain. But she wouldn't answer. She was adrift, floating in some darkness I couldn't reach. I used to think of it like a river, something black and endless, pulling her further and further away from me. I hated her for

that. I hated her more when she came back —
wild-eyed and ravenous, desperation clawing its
way out of her skin. She'd scream sometimes,
accuse me of things I didn't understand. She'd
search the apartment with frantic hands, tearing
through drawers and closets, ripping the
cushions from the couch. Always looking for
more. Always hungry. It scared me how
predictable it became. I could time it. I could feel
it coming.

I started writing things down just to make sense
of it. Words that came to me when the world got
too quiet, when her breathing was too soft and I
was left alone with thoughts that felt bigger than I
was. I wrote them because I was afraid of
forgetting. I wrote them because I was afraid of
remembering.

Diary Entry - January 22, 1977

Mama fell asleep again. It's the
bad sleep. The kind where her
eyes stay open but she don't see
nothing. Her mouth hangs open
like she's trying to talk but the
words all got stuck in her throat.

I tried shaking her but she won't move. I put my hand on her chest and felt her breathing so she's not dead. I kept talking to her but she just stared at the wall like it was made of gold or something. I whispered in her ear, just in case she couldn't hear me. Told her it was morning. Told her I was hungry. But she didn't move. Didn't blink. I thought maybe she got stuck.

I hate when she sleeps like this. I hate the men who come around and leave their bottles and dirty fingers everywhere. I hate the smell of the smoke she likes so much. It makes my eyes burn.

I wish she'd wake up. I wish we had real food. I wish I could run away and never come back.

But then she came. Mama was still asleep and that woman, one of the ladies always sniffing around for leftovers, came into my room. She smelled like flowers. Not real

ones—the kind that come from
bottles. Her breath was sweet and
sharp, like the drinks the men
brought with them. She smiled at
me like we were playing a game.

She told me to be quiet. Told me it
was our little secret. Her hands
were cold and rough. It hurt. I
wanted to scream, but my mouth
wouldn't work. My voice stayed
trapped in my throat, like hers.
She laughed when I cried.

After, she patted my head and
told me I was a good boy. I tried
to tell Mama after. Whispered it in
her ear. But she just stared. She
didn't hear me. I don't think she
ever did. Mama never woke up.
She just kept staring at nothing.

I hope she never comes back.

That night never left me. It buried something
inside me—something that once trusted, once
believed. I learned that silence could protect you.
Or destroy you.

The darkness surrounded me like a cocoon. The way her hands felt like ice, and the cruel smile that curled her lips when I whimpered. I was too young to understand what she was doing, but old enough to know it was wrong.

Something inside me snapped. A part of me that had once felt fear now boiled with a hatred so pure it seared my veins.

That was the first time I wished for death. Hers. Mine. Anyone's.

But the anger only grew. It grew until it consumed me. It became a fire that burned through my veins, its heat scalding away the innocence that once clung to me like a tattered cloak.

It was the night I realized I was alone. Alone and powerless.

The world had taken everything from me. And I would take something from the world.

It wasn't just rage. It was something far colder, coiled and patient. A desire not only to hurt but to reclaim what had been taken. The helplessness

I'd known seeped into my bones, hardening to something sharp and unyielding.

I remembered her laughter—how it scraped against my ears, raw and callous. Her fingers, jagged things that gripped me like roots tearing through stone. Her voice, cloying and brittle, feeding on my pain like a parasite savoring its host.

Her skin, pale and ghostly, seemed to gleam under the dim light. It made her look clean, almost pure, like she didn't belong in the decay she wandered. But her eyes were sunken, drained of everything except the need to consume.

Terror and fury tangled within me, knotting into something fierce and unforgiving. My mother lay comatose, swallowed by her own poison—lost in a haze she chose over me. She was supposed to protect me. But she couldn't even be bothered to save herself.

The world had taught me its lesson early— survival belonged to the ruthless. I couldn't rely on her. I couldn't rely on anyone.

The days that followed blurred into shadows. I withdrew into myself, the simmering rage curling around me like smoke. I stopped speaking to my mother, stopped trying to wake her when she slipped too deep into her poison.

Walls rose around me, thick and impenetrable. I convinced myself that pain was power, that suffering could be wielded like a blade. And when I looked at my mother, I saw only weakness—something to despise.

The woman who hurt me never returned. But it didn't matter. The damage had been done. Innocence was a luxury I could no longer afford. Something darker had taken its place, whispering to me whenever the nights grew too quiet.

I wasn't just angry anymore. I was changed.

My childhood had been stolen from me. But I would take something back.

"Train up a child in the way he should go, and when he is old he will not depart from it," my grandfather used to say, his voice heavy with conviction during Sunday services. He would rest his hand on my shoulder, squeezing gently as if to make sure the words sank deep. "You remember that, boy. God don't forget his own."

School was another kind of torment. I was smart—I knew that much. Teachers scribbled words like "gifted" and "bright" on papers I barely glanced at. Praise that rang echoing when the world outside their classrooms remained indifferent.

But intelligence meant nothing when I couldn't show up. When my mother's binges locked her away for days and I was left scavenging for scraps. When the only meals I had were crusts fished from the neighbors' trash or stolen candy bars from the corner store.

I repeated a grade. Not because I didn't understand the lessons, but because I missed too many days to pass. I watched children younger than me move forward, smiling with parents who waited for them outside the school doors. Parents who embraced them. Fed them.

A teacher asked me once why I was always so tired. Why I had bruises I couldn't explain, and dark circles etched beneath my eyes. The truth was too sharp, so I softened it. Said I was clumsy. Said I stayed up late reading because I liked books. Part of that was true.

Books became my escape, a world untouched by the infection that consumed everything else. Stories of heroes and villains. Of revenge and justice. I devoured every page like a starving animal, savoring the power those words held. They made me feel something beyond hunger and neglect. They made me believe I could be something more than a child lost to the streets of Philadelphia.

I had almost convinced myself she was dead. Gone. A ghost fading into the cracks of my memory. But ghosts don't disappear. They wait. They hide. And they always come back.

March 1980. She was back, prowling the same streets with that familiar, fractured hunger in her eyes. Thinner. Gaunt. The bones of her face protruding like knives beneath paper-thin skin.

But her smile was the same. That sick, knowing smirk that made my blood run cold.

I followed her. She lived in a squalid apartment not far from where I scraped by. A place as broken as she was. The door hung slightly open when I arrived, left ajar by either carelessness or desperation. Inside, the air hung heavy with stale cigarettes and a dampness that seeped into the plaster, clinging to the walls like a fevered memory. The walls were yellowed with smoke stains, the floor sticky beneath my shoes. A thin layer of dust coated everything, like the place had been abandoned by hope long before she ever stepped inside.

My heartbeat crashed against my ribs, each pulse like a countdown, steady and unyielding. The hallway leading to her apartment felt longer than it should have, stretching out like it was daring me to turn back. I almost did—twice. But something heavier than fear kept me moving. Something that tasted like iron and felt like a promise.

The door was cracked, the stale scent of neglect and torment spilling into the hallway. I pushed it open. It groaned on its hinges, loud enough that she should have looked up. But she didn't. She was slouched on that ratty couch, a syringe cradled in her hand, flame dancing beneath the spoon, eyes glossy and far away. I'd seen that look before—lost to the haze, drifting somewhere I couldn't follow. Somewhere I never wanted to.

For a moment, I just watched her. Watched the way her hands steadied as she cooked the poison, watched the way her lips moved—soft murmurs like she was praying. I stepped forward, the floorboards creaking beneath my weight, and she snapped out of it, eyes locking onto mine. Her pupils shrank, and I saw the shift—the moment she remembered.

Her lips twisted into a sneer. "Ah, it's you," she spat, voice crackling like static. The needle wavered in her hand, but she didn't drop it. Her eyes narrowed, and I could see the hate simmering beneath the surface, always just a breath away. "What's the matter, baby boy? Come to play again?"

I swallowed hard, the room tilting slightly. "I came to—" I didn't know how to finish. I didn't even know why I was there, but the words were spilling out anyway. "I came to..."

I was too nervous to get it out. I didn't even know what I wanted. I had no plan. But something pushed me forward, step by step, as if the hallway were moving and I was just a passenger. My hands were shaking, palms slick with sweat, but I couldn't stop. Not now. Not anymore.

She laughed, brittle and sharp. "What? Came to what? Oh, you want more of the last time?" Her grin spread wider, teeth yellowed and uneven.

"You enjoyed it, didn't you? You didn't say a word. Just watched." Her eyes glimmered with something cruel. "Don't pretend you're innocent."

My vision blurred. I took a step back, but she followed, the needle still pinched between her fingers. "What, you gonna cry? Little boy all grown up and still a bitch?" she hissed, stepping closer. "You think you can just walk in here and—"

I didn't hear the rest. My gaze broke from her eyes and fell on the cluttered table by the wall. That's when I saw it—propped against the wall, half-hidden beneath a stack of yellowed newspapers and discarded bottles. A University of Pennsylvania diploma. The glass was cracked, spiderwebbing through her name, and a thin layer of dust clung to its surface. It looked like it hadn't been touched in years. Like something she had forgotten, just like everything else.

I stared at it for a moment, a reminder of something she could have been. Something she never became. All that promise sealed in glass, left to spoil beside empty bottles and burnt spoons. The weight of it settled on me, heavy and suffocating, the kind of weight you can't shake off. She must have seen me looking because she laughed, brittle and sharp.

"Oh, you like that?" she sneered, catching my gaze. "Look at you, acting like you understand. That piece of paper don't mean shit." Her eyes gleamed with something like pride. "You think I give a damn about that? All that was just a game. This—" she raised the syringe in her hand, fingers trembling, "—this is the only thing that's real."

Her footsteps moved closer. Her voice got louder. "What's the matter? You gonna cry like you did before? Little bitch can't even—"

I moved before I realized I was moving. My hand wrapped around the handle of the knife, its weight familiar, almost comforting. I turned, and she stopped mid-step, eyes locked on mine. For a heartbeat, we just stood there—her eyes flicking between my face and the blade in my hand. Then she laughed.

"Look at you," she taunted. "Think you're a man now? Gonna do something about it?" She took another step forward, and I felt my grip tighten. Her hand reached out, fingers stained and trembling, and something inside me snapped.

The blade went in easier than I expected. There was almost no resistance. Her breath hitched, and she looked at me like I'd betrayed her. Her mouth opened and closed, but no sound came out. I watched her eyes flicker, the way the light dimmed and faded, replaced by something empty. I didn't stop. I couldn't stop. The rhythm of it took over—automatic, disconnected. I felt the weight of each motion, but not the guilt. Her screams sputtered and choked, swallowed by the quiet that followed.

When it was over, I stepped back, chest heaving, knife still slick in my hand. Her body laid mangled on the floor, eyes staring up at the ceiling like she was still searching for the answer to a question she'd never asked. The silence stretched, thin and taut, like a wire waiting to snap. But it didn't. Nothing moved. The diploma lay shattered beside her, a piece of glass jutting out like it had tried to escape. The words, 'University of Pennsylvania,' were still visible beneath the dust and blood. A symbol of everything she could have been, and everything she had thrown away.

The universe adjusted to her absence with indifference. Not even a flicker. Not even a breath. Like she had never mattered at all. And for the first time, I understood what it meant to disappear.

I left her apartment as quietly as I had entered. Outside, I used the neighbor's hose to wash the blood from my hands, arms, and face. It felt like shedding old skin, peeling away the remnants of what I used to be. Each splash of water stripped something away, revealing something sharper, colder beneath. I watched the pink streams fade, swallowed by the gutter, until only the cold bite of the hose remained. It felt like a baptism—like I was scrubbing away the last traces of who I had been. I watched the pink streams fade, swallowed by the gutter, until only the cold bite of the hose remained. The water was frigid, biting against my skin. When the water stopped, it was as if everything stilled, like the whole world paused to watch. Not the stillness of fear, but of finality. Like the chaos inside had been muted, its whispers replaced by something clearer, something certain.

Looking back, I still wonder if it was always that easy, or if it just felt that way because of what she represented. That first kill wasn't just about revenge—it was the unraveling of something deeper. I used to tell myself it was justice, a reckoning for what she'd done to me. But that night, as I washed the blood from my hands and watched it spiral down the drain, I realized it was more than that. It was control. It was power. For the first time, I wasn't just surviving—I was deciding who did. And that kind of power, it doesn't leave you. It lingers, curling itself around your thoughts, whispering that it's yours to take whenever you want. I told myself it was righteous. But I know now that was just the lie I needed to believe.

No one noticed me. No one cared. I slipped back into my room and let the silence settle over me like a shroud. The world had finally heard me. And I wasn't finished speaking.

The next morning, I listened to the radio, read the paper as best I could. Her death was nothing more than a passing note, buried beneath headlines of a mobster gunned down. Angelo Bruno, they called him. His name screamed from the pages. Her life was reduced to two sentences—an echo swallowed by the city's noise. But that was fine. I didn't do it for them. I did it for me. But for the first time, I understood. Power wasn't in the act; it was in being remembered. Even if she wasn't, I was.

Her name was already ash. Just a mention of a woman found dead in her apartment. Stabbed to death.

No one looked for her. No one looked for me. I could do it again. And again. I could become the shadow that moved through their lives, slipping through the cracks, unseen and untouched. Power wasn't just in the act—it was in how easily the world forgot. And I could make them forget, again and again.

I whispered it under my breath, the words slipping through clenched teeth: "O Lord, God of vengeance; O God of vengeance, shine forth." The words tasted like iron on my tongue—sharp and metallic, lingering even after the whisper faded.

This was my first kill.

And it felt like salvation.

Poem - The Bliss of Blood

I tasted God in the silence of
death,
A baptism of crimson, the warmth
of her breath.
Steel slid clean through sinew and

bone,
Her screams were the choir, her
blood was my throne.

The night split open, a wound in
the dark,
Her agony painted, my indelible
mark.
No mercy, no guilt, only
pleasure's embrace,
As life ebbed away from her pale,
twisted face.

I watched her convulse, a puppet
undone,
Her terror a hymn, her suffering
won.
Each plunge of the blade, a pulse
of delight,
An ecstasy sharper than hunger or
fright.

This was creation, destruction
made pure,
A rapture so savage, so vile yet
sure.
Her blood was the ink, her pain
was the script,

> A gospel of slaughter, my sanity
> slipped.
>
> I craved it again, the violence and
> thrill,
> A hunger unending, a void I must
> fill.
> For only in death could I feel
> something true,
> The bliss of her ruin, the darkness
> I drew.

The sensation coiled through me, consuming everything else. It was power. It was release. It was mine.

I'd seen them—the addicts who stumbled into my mother's apartment, trembling with desperation, their eyes glazing over as poison pulled them under. The groans and slackened bodies, the trough bliss they chased like beggars clawing at something sacred.

Their highs were pale imitations. Fleeting numbness that dulled pain only to have it return sharper, hungrier. What I'd found was something purer. Absolute.

Nothing had ever wanted me. Nothing had ever made me feel whole. Until the blood pooled around her, and I stood there, breathless, feeling alive.

I clung to that euphoria, hoarded it like stolen treasure. The control was mine alone, fierce, and unending. More complete than any high I'd ever witnessed.

But even as I replayed the moment over and over, something buried deep clawed its way back.

I was younger then. Too young to understand the meaning of pain or betrayal. It was a Sunday morning, and my grandparents had taken me to church. Sunlight spilled through the stained glass, painting the pews in hues of sapphire and ruby. Back then, I believed salvation was something you prayed for. A whispered promise held tight between clasped hands. But now, I understood — it wasn't given. It was taken. Ripped from the hands of those who never saw it coming.

The preacher spoke of innocence that day. How children were God's most precious creation. Pure, unblemished, untouched by the corruption of the world. The preacher said the pure in heart would see God. I wondered if I already had.

I held my grandmother's hand and believed every word.

Now, years later, I wondered what purity even meant. How could anyone claim I was innocent when the darkness had already swallowed me whole? How could I be pure when blood had become my only truth?

The preacher's words felt like a mockery. Innocence was a lie. Something meant for children who never had to see the things I'd seen. Who never had to survive the way I had.

Purity was a luxury I could never afford. I had traded it for something real—something solid. Innocence was a ghost, something fragile and fleeting. But power? Power was mine. It stayed. It lingered. It became a part of me.

But power—that was real. Control—that was salvation. It wasn't just an act; it was a sacrament. A ritual of becoming. Every blade a prayer, every drop of blood an offering.

The memory of the church faded, drowned out by the satisfaction I now clung to. Whatever innocence I might have once possessed was long dead.

And I didn't mourn it. I had found salvation—not in forgiveness, not in redemption, but in the permanence of power.

Purity wasn't something you were born with. It wasn't a gift; it was a blade you forged yourself, cutting away the weak and the broken until only strength remained.

Power had replaced purity. It slipped into my veins like molten iron, filling the hollows where innocence once lived. I had found a new truth—sharpened and absolute.

Where the preachers spoke of salvation beyond death, I discovered mine through the act itself. Where they found God in the light, I found Him in the dark. In the moments where breath slipped away and silence reigned. My salvation wasn't in forgiveness—it was in fear.

Her blood still clung to my hands, the scent of it thick and unyielding. I replayed it over and over—the way the blade sank in, the way the world held its breath. Control. For the first time, I had seized it. For the first time, the world bent to my will.

But the hunger remained. Relentless. Insatiable. It gnawed at me, whispering promises in the quiet spaces of my mind, urging me to reclaim that power.

I thought of the preacher's words—that the pure in heart would see God. Maybe I hadn't seen Him yet. But I would. Someday. One blade at a time.

I knew I would listen again. I could feel it coiling inside me, that craving for silence. Because salvation wasn't written in scripture—it was carved in flesh. It wasn't spoken from pulpits—it was whispered in the moments where breath stilled and blood cooled. It was written in fear. And I was ready to read it again.

THOU SHALT FEED THE PAIN

September 1980

Before dawn, I woke expecting cake or a gift; instead, the apartment was silent—counters cold and bare, stray frosting crumbs on the floor, and the stale scent of old coffee hanging in the air. My footsteps echoed in the stillness, dust catching in the slivers of morning light. I checked the kitchen drawers, one after another, until I found a lone birthday candle—blue and half-melted from last year. I held it for a moment, its wick frayed and bent, then placed it back and shut the drawer. Even the small act of hope felt like a lie.

I turned twelve this day. September 3rd. My birthday.

Twelve should've meant something—another step away from the broken child I'd always been. I remembered her laughter in the sun as she promised a trip to the park, her hair glowing like copper—then I was here, back in this empty apartment, the promise broken.

I planned it out so many times. Waking up to the smell of pancakes on the stove, my mother humming softly in the kitchen. Maybe she'd have a surprise for me—something wrapped in cheap paper with my name scrawled across the top. We'd go to the park, just the two of us, her pushing me on the swings like she used to before everything fell apart. I imagined us stopping for ice cream, the kind that dripped down your hand faster than you could eat it. She'd tell me stories, the kind she used to tell when her eyes were still bright, when her laugh didn't sound like it hurt.

Mrs. Ellison's door creaked open across the hall. She'd been there for as long as I could remember, always looking out through the crack of her doorway, eyes sharp and glassy. Her son died young—a needle in his arm before he ever reached twenty. She never talked about him, but the photos on her wall were enough: birthdays, summer days at the shore, faces frozen in time before addiction stole them away.

When my mother first moved us in, Mrs. Ellison would bring over leftovers. Spaghetti mostly. Sometimes she'd linger by the door after handing it over, her voice just above a whisper: 'You got enough food, boy?' or 'You need anything? You know I'm just across the hall.' I'd nod, always the same reply: 'I'm fine, Mrs. Ellison.'

As the years went on, she brought less. Her fridge grew emptier, her steps slower. Sometimes she'd linger at my door after handing me a plate of spaghetti, like she wanted to say something more, but the words never came. Her eyes would flicker, mouth opening just slightly before she'd catch herself, nod, and shuffle back to her apartment. But every year on my birthday, she'd slide a card under my door. I remember thanking her once, the words slipping out before I could think twice. She just nodded, eyes glassy, her hand still on the doorframe for a moment longer than usual. Then she turned away, shuffling back to her apartment, the silence folding in behind her. It was always the same — "Happy Birthday" written in shaky cursive, sometimes with a dollar bill folded inside if she could spare it. Her pity settled in the silence, colder than the empty room.

Instead, I spent my birthday the way I spent most days—wandering the city, drifting past boarded-up shops, empty playgrounds, and families that moved like shadows through cracked windows. I watched kids playing in front yards, their laughter muffled by the glass that separated me from their world. I tried to fill the emptiness that gnawed at me, but it only grew sharper, hungrier.

I hadn't been the same since March. Since her. Church was harder now—every Sunday, I'd sit on that hard wooden pew and listen to the preacher talk about redemption and forgiveness, his voice a low rumble that shook the walls. I wanted to believe it, to think that what I did was evil, that it was sin—but it didn't feel like that. It felt good. It felt like the knife belonged in my hand, like it was a part of me I didn't know I needed. Sometimes I'd hear her voice in my head, whispering curses and laughing that shrill laugh that made my skin crawl. But other times, it was silent. Peaceful. And that's when I knew it was right. I changed that day—not because of what I did, but because of how it felt. I wanted that feeling back. I craved it like air, like a heartbeat I hadn't realized I'd lost. To feel in control once again.

That moment twisted me into something I couldn't recognize. And on my birthday, I couldn't shake the thought that I had been remade that day. Not in September. But in March. When I took her life and felt the purity of violence course through me.

The need hadn't gone away. If anything, it had grown sharper. Hungrier.

That hunger wasn't just a craving; it was a rebellion—a force that rose up to fill the hollowness she left behind. I didn't recognize it at first. It started as a whisper, something I could ignore if I tried hard enough. But it grew louder, more insistent, clawing its way through my thoughts like roots cracking through concrete. It thrived in the quiet moments, stretching itself out, reminding me of its presence. It was more than a need; it was a reckoning. A promise of control in a world that had always denied it. For so long, I'd been powerless—an unwilling spectator in my own life, watching as others inflicted pain with impunity. But now, I understood. Power didn't come from prayer or promises; it came from the ability to take. To end. To decide when the stillness would come. And with each passing day, that need grew sharper, more focused. It wasn't enough to remember it—I needed to feel it again. That rush. That finality. Because for the first time, I understood what it meant to be more than a victim. I understood what it meant to own fear.

Was this what addiction felt like? I'd watched it twist her, seen it hollow out her eyes, turn her hands to trembling husks. I used to wonder why she kept going back to it, why she crawled through hell just to taste that feeling again. But I didn't wonder anymore. I understood. That surge of power wasn't just something I wanted. It was something I needed. I could feel it pulsing beneath my skin, curling around my bones, waiting. Maybe it had always been there. Maybe I'd just been too afraid to reach for it.

And now I was twelve. Another year older. Another year deeper into this new understanding. I wasn't moving toward innocence. I was moving further away from it.

School started the next day. Sixth grade. Middle school. A new beginning, they called it. A chance to grow and make friends.

But for me, it was just another cage. Another place to pretend I was normal.

This first day of school was different. Hallways crammed with bodies, voices crashing together until they became nothing but noise. The teachers smiled and handed out textbooks. Talked about goals and standards. The chalk scraped across the board, the scent of dust lingering in the stale classroom air.

None of it mattered. Even surrounded by life, I felt the hunger simmer beneath my skin.

I sat at my desk, my fingers tracing the wood's grain, eyes drifting over faces bright with eagerness. Parents arriving outside the building, kissing foreheads and telling their children to have a good day.

I didn't have that. Only the memory of her. The knife. The blood.

My teacher, Mrs. Johnson tried to draw me out, asking me about my summer—where I'd gone, what I'd done, who I'd spent it with. "Did you go with family?" she asked, her eyes searching mine. "Did you have fun?" Her questions sat between us, heavy and waiting. I just nodded, gave her what she wanted—easy answers, simple stories that didn't ask questions back.

Lies rolled off my tongue like second nature. I told her I spent the summer at my grandparents' house, that I went to the beach. Simple stories. Safe ones.

But my eyes kept slipping to the windows. To the world outside. To places where I could be alone, unbothered, and unseen.

I couldn't concentrate. Couldn't care about math or spelling or the rules Mrs. Johnson scrawled on the chalkboard. My mind was already retreating, slipping away before the lunch bell even rang.

Lunch was chaos. A mess of voices and bodies shoving past each other. I took a spot at the edge of the cafeteria, back against the wall where I could see everything. Halfway through an expired fruit cup I found in the trash, David walked in. He moved through the chaos like he owned it, weaving between tables with a grin and a handshake. I watched him laugh with friends I only dreamed of having, like he belonged to a world I could only watch from the outside. People leaned in when he laughed, like they wanted to be part of it. His voice carried across the room, easy and unburdened. I first noticed him during attendance. His name came right before mine—David Powell. "Present!" He said it loud, with honor like he wanted to make sure everyone heard it. He sat two rows up, leaning back in his chair, cracking jokes with the kid next to him. When my name was called, I just mumbled 'Here' and stared back down at the desk. He must have noticed me watching. He plopped down across from me like he'd been doing it for years, like the seat belonged to him.

"Powell and Powers," he said, grinning. "Gotta stick together, right? Saw you looking down in class. Now here you are, tucked in the corner like you're trying to disappear. I get it. I've been there. Figured I'd keep my roll-call buddy company." He laughed like it was the funniest thing in the world.

"You look like you've seen a ghost," he said, smiling as if the world was his to play with.

He studied me for a second, and gestured half of his sandwich, like he was waiting for me to make a move. I just stared at it, half-expecting him to pull it back or laugh like it was some kind of joke. But he didn't. He just slid it across the table, his eyes steady and unbothered.

"You looked hungry," he said casually, nudging it closer. "My mom always says you can't think straight on an empty stomach. Figured I'd help you out."

I waited a beat too long before reaching for it, the crust rough under my fingers. It was real. He was real. And I wasn't sure what to do with that.

"Stick with me, kid," he said with a smirk "Or don't. But it'll be more fun if you do." He beamed, eyes glimmering with something bright and reckless. "Do you even laugh? Might break your face, but it's worth a shot. Guess it's easier for some of us," he added, his grin slipping for just a heartbeat. "But I'm stubborn. One day, I'll make you laugh."

Something so simple it felt foreign. He called it a meal. I called it mercy.

We didn't say much that first day. Just chewed and listened to the noise around us. But something about him felt steady, like he belonged to a world I hadn't touched in a long time.

"Why'd you sit here?" I finally asked on day three.

He shrugged, sipping his milk. "You looked like someone who needed a real friend."

I stared at him, uncertain how to respond.

"Don't get weird—I don't like you like that," he added quickly, flashing that crooked grin. "I've just been the kid in the corner too. I know the look."

That should've embarrassed me. Instead, it settled something inside.

David never asked questions about my home, my clothes, or the silence I wore like a shield. He just showed up, like a habit I didn't know I needed.

He reminded me of who I might've been in a different life—one with sunlight and sleep and peanut butter that wasn't stale. Not a soulmate. Not a savior. Just a boy who saw through the quiet. And for a while, that was enough.

After that, David was just… there. Every lunch period, sliding into the seat across from me like it was his place to be. His words cut through the noise, careless and steady. "Maybe you're just waiting for someone to finally tell you your fly's been down all week," he said once, leaning back with a grin. I looked down instinctively, and his laughter erupted—sharp and unrestrained. He nearly choked on his sandwich, his face red from laughing.

"Man, you actually checked!" he said, wiping his eyes. "I didn't think I'd get you that easy. Guess you do have a sense of humor somewhere in there."

I tried not to smile, but it slipped out, small and unguarded. He caught it and pointed. "See? Progress," he said, still grinning. "Told you I'd get you to crack one day."

He made me laugh. Sometimes.

He laughed like I was someone worth knowing. "See you tomorrow," he'd say, like it was a promise he intended to keep. But even as David laughed, the sound couldn't reach where I was sinking. His words were like sunlight pushing against a locked door. I'd smile back sometimes, just enough to make him believe his kindness was breaking through. But the truth was, my thoughts were already pulling me away—back to the silence that waited for me at home. Back to the hunger that never left.

His presence became something to anchor me when everything else felt out of reach. But even as David's words pulled me back into the world, something in me stayed locked away—caged where even kindness couldn't reach.

No matter how much I tried to bury it, the drive simmered beneath the surface, restless and waiting. Even David's kindness couldn't quiet it. Nothing could.

Walking home was a blur of noise and shadow, the city's pulse thrumming against my ears. I'd pass homes with lit windows, mothers calling their kids in for dinner, the glow of lights spilling out onto the snow. I wondered if they even saw me out here, or if I was just another shadow slipping by. I tried to imagine what it would feel like to step inside one, to feel warm.

The apartment swallowed light; curtains pulled tight as if night had crept inside. The air clung to everything, stale and bitter, as if neglect had settled into the walls like mold.

Most days, my mother wasn't there. Sometimes I'd find her sprawled across the couch, eyes half-closed, lost to whatever high she'd chased. Other times she'd be gone for days, leaving me to scrounge whatever scraps were left.

The apartment devoured sound, its quiet pressing down like a weight. I moved through it like a trespasser, waiting for something to break.

The urge lay buried, smoldering beneath the surface, feeding on wounds that refused to heal. I knew it wouldn't stay buried for long.

Everything felt colder at home. Heavy, like a suffocating blanket drawn too tight. The apartment had become a cemetery, and I was the only living thing left to haunt it.

I tried to focus on school. On David and his effortless laughter. On the assignments that should've kept my mind busy. But the yearning followed me everywhere, a parasite feeding on my thoughts.

Sometimes I would hear my mother's voice from the couch, slurred and cracked like shattered glass. She'd ask me where I'd been or bark at me to get her something from the deli. Cigarettes. Beer. Pills if I knew where to find them.

Other times she'd say nothing at all. Just lay there, her eyes half-open and glazed over, staring at something I couldn't see. I'd talk to her, and she wouldn't respond, her chest rising and falling in shallow, uneven breaths.

When she was awake and coherent enough to notice me, she'd tell me she loved me. Her words tangled in guilt and desperation, as if she was trying to convince herself it was true.

But the kindness never lasted. It always decayed into accusations, blaming me for things I never did or words I never said. Her anger was erratic, unpredictable. Like everything else in that decaying apartment.

I started staying out later. Wandering the streets until the sky bruised black and the city's ugliness crept from its hiding places. I'd pass alleyways where addicts hunched over like broken animals, their voices trembling with longing of their own.

I wondered if I looked like them. If my addiction made me just as lost.

I tried to quiet it. Tried to bury it beneath the routine of school, the forced conversations with

David, the isolation of my own thoughts. But it was always there.

The need. The appetite. And the memory of that night.

I would sit by the window sometimes, watching the streetlights flicker in the darkness. Listening to the sounds of the city—sirens wailing in the distance, laughter bleeding into screams, the low hum of desperation that vibrated beneath it all.

I felt like a reflection, watching life pass by from the wrong side of a pane of glass.

I wondered if she could feel it too. If her high had taken her so far away that she was trapped, just like me.

Something was growing inside of me, and I knew it wouldn't leave me alone. I called it the hunger.

Diary Entry - December 19, 1980

> Almost Christmas. The teachers
> keep talking about family and
> presents like it's supposed to
> matter. They made us write
> down what we're thankful for. I

just stared at the paper until they
told us to hand it in.

I don't even know if I feel
anything anymore. Just
this…thing inside me that keeps
me up at night. Like it's trying to
crawl out of me.

David keeps saying I should go
to the basketball game with him.
He thinks jokes and peanut
butter and banana sandwiches
can fix anything.

I wish it could.

I can't remember her voice when
she's not yelling or crying or
passed out.

Sometimes I just wait for her to
look at me. Really look at me. But
she's always somewhere else.
Lost in her own mess.

I keep reading that verse over
and over. When justice is done, it
brings joy to the righteous but

terror to evildoers.
I don't know if I'm good or bad.
Just that whatever's inside me is
getting worse. I don't want it to
get worse.

Christmas break came quick, like time was running from me. Two weeks of freedom, the teachers called it. David was excited, talking about how his family planned to spend the holidays at his grandmother's house. Presents, food, laughter. All the things that were just words to me.

My breath fogged in the bitter air as I walked home alone, each step heavier than the last, the chill settling into my bones like a warning. The city felt colder than usual, its edges sharpened by the chill that seeped into my bone

When I reached the apartment, The door hung open just a crack, enough to whisper danger but not enough to see. It creaked with every shift of the wind, like it was breathing. A voice in the darkness beckoned me to push it open, luring me closer with a weight I didn't yet understand.

Inside, everything was quiet. That kind of silence that doesn't just fill the room—it swallows it whole, like sound itself had been devoured. It was the stillness of something waiting, something patient and unyielding.

I stepped forward, the silence growing heavier, thick as smoke. My eyes adjusted to the darkness, shapes emerging slowly—first the corner of the coffee table, then the edge of the couch, and then...her. My mother lay dismantled on the living room floor, a fractured shadow stretched across rotting carpet. Her face was swollen and bruised, blood caked along her lips and chin, her eyes half-open, staring at nothing. Her arms were twisted beneath her like discarded limbs of a broken marionette, strings cut and forgotten.

I stared at her, the world narrowing to the ruined mess of her body. Her clothes were torn, skin marred by purple and yellow bruises, dried blood staining her hair.

A voice from behind me broke the silence.

"She owed him money. A lot of it. Screamed at him, told him to get out. So, he beat her. Just kept going until...well..."

I turned to see Mrs. Ellison. Her voice was low, thick with fear.

"No one called the cops," she continued. "Ain't nobody gonna call the cops around here," she whispered, her eyes flicking to the walls like they had ears.

I looked back at my mother's body. The hunger stirred, the coldness creeping in and numbing everything else.

I left the apartment and walked to the nearest payphone. Gathered myself and dialed the police.

"My neighbor's dead in her apartment," I said, my voice flat and empty.

"What's your name, son?" the operator asked.

I gave the address, my voice hollow and distant, like it belonged to someone else. "And your name?" she asked again. Her voice crackled through the receiver, thin and far away. I didn't answer. My hand slipped from the phone, letting it dangle by its cord. I heard her voice still sputtering from the receiver, calling out for me, but I just stood there, watching it sway back and forth, like it would never stop.

The police came. They took her away. I never saw her again. No funeral. No goodbye. Just the echo of sirens fading into the night.

She was gone, and all that remained was the emptiness. Her absence carved out something inside me, left a hollow space that only one thing could fill.

A ravenous void gnawing at the edges of my sanity, a beast starved of peace and swollen with rage. It fed on grief and grew stronger, thrashing against my ribs like caged lightning. The world had fractured, and all that was left were the jagged pieces it tore through me.

I could feel her absence like a wound too deep to heal. The air tasted of rust and regret, her blood still staining my memory as if it seeped into the marrow of my bones.

The hunger was a whisper and a roar. It spoke to me in verses, scripture twisted into something sharp and unforgiving.

I repeated Psalm 58:10 over and over again, "The righteous will rejoice when he sees the vengeance; he will bathe his feet in the blood of the wicked." Letting the words weave through me until they became part of the deprivation's voice. A symphony of wrath and righteousness.

I wanted him to suffer. I wanted his blood to spill like hers had. To feel the pain, I carried every time I closed my eyes.

It consumed me.

I stalked the streets with eyes that burned for shadows, for tales of the monster hiding in plain sight. I listened to whispers carried by the wind, piecing together fragments of conversations like shattered glass.

Every alley held a promise. Every darkened corner a possibility. I would find him. I would drag him into the cold, unforgiving light and make him pay.

And when I do, I would feed the famine.

The world had stolen from me, left me hollow and burning. The need to feed my vengeance was the only thing that made sense anymore.

But sometimes, in the quiet spaces between rage and despair, I would remember her kindness. The softness of her voice when she sang to me before sleep, her lullabies clinging to me like warmth in the dead of night. The way her arms would wrap around me on nights when the cold seeped through the walls, her embrace the only shield against a world that felt too large and hostile.

I could still hear her laughter echoing through the years. Laughter that rang like silver bells when she was sober, unburdened by the poison she poured into her veins. Those days were rare, but their beauty made them feel eternal.

She'd brush my hair and call me handsome. Tell me stories about her own childhood, of summers spent by the river with her brothers, splashing and laughing until the sun dipped below the trees. She'd promise me that one day we'd have a house of our own, far away from the concrete and decay. A place with green grass and flowers she'd plant herself.

I tried to hold onto those moments, the good ones untouched by the disease that tore her apart. Before her eyes grew dull and her words slurred with the poison she couldn't escape. Before the drugs sunk their claws into her and left her a hollow shell.

I wondered how different things could have been if she had fought harder. If she had gotten clean and stayed that way. If the Mother I remembered from those fleeting good days had been strong enough to survive the darkness that swallowed her whole.

Maybe she would have been proud of me. Maybe she would have found a way to love me without pain tangled in every word.

Maybe we could have had that house she always dreamed about.

But she was gone. And my appetite remained.

I stalked the streets with an obsession that felt like starvation and prayer fused together. Mornings and nights dissolved into a fevered haze of pursuit and longing. I barely slept, eyes wide and wild, fueled by a rage that throbbed beneath my skin.

I clung to scraps of information, the words of men on corners and the drunken confessions spilled in shadowed alleys.

But I kept searching. Relentless. Driven. Every time I closed my eyes, I saw her face bruised and broken, her body balled up on the floor like something discarded and forgotten.

David didn't disappear.

I made him fade.

Every time he tried to reach me, I met him with silence or scorn, like kindness was something I no longer deserved. I watched the light in his eyes dim, not out of anger—but confusion.

The cafeteria felt bigger without him, the world stretching out like a wasteland. I didn't need light anymore. I needed purpose.

I drifted through the days like a feather in the wind. Detached from everything but the craving. When David stopped sitting across from me, I realized I had carved him out, just like I did everything else that made me feel alive.

Sometimes I missed him. Not his jokes or his food, but the weight of his presence—proof that someone, once, had cared enough to show up without asking for anything back. But by then, it was too late.

I wasn't the boy he sat with anymore.

I was something else—something hungrier.

And I was alone.

So I filled that loneliness with purpose. A mission. I would find the man who killed her. He hadn't just taken her—he'd stolen everything. David. The light he brought to the edge of my darkness. The sliver of hope I thought might still be mine.

He snuffed it out.

He shattered it like glass under his boot, leaving only shards that cut deeper with every step. Hope wasn't just lost. It was murdered.

I would drag him from whatever filthy hole he called home. I would make him bleed. His wickedness would devour him. His sins would catch up with him, dragging him down just like he did to me.

Their sins would consume them. Their wickedness would rise up like shadows and devour them whole. The Lord would wipe them out, that's what the scripture promised.

And I had nothing left to hold onto. Not light. Not kindness. Not even hope. Just the vow. I whispered the words like a prayer forged in iron. A promise branded on my soul. He would suffer. He would pay. His own darkness would drag him under, just like it did to me.

That was the only thing I had left.

THOU SHALT REPAY BLOOD WITH BLOOD

Summer 1983

Letter to Mom

You're gone. And I'm still here.
Picking through scraps and
shadows. The world's already
moved on, like you were just
some junkie nobody cared about.

I talk to you in the dark, hoping
you can hear me wherever you
ended up. Maybe you're just
another ghost roaming the same

filthy streets. Or maybe you're just gone.

I remember pieces of you. The real you. Before the drugs twisted you up and left you hollow. Before you started looking at me like I was something you had to deal with instead of your kid.

People say you were weak. That you chose it. But I saw how it tore you up. How you fought it until you couldn't anymore. I saw what it did to you—turned your kindness into rage, your laughter into some broken, hollow thing.

It wasn't your fault. But you left me anyway.

I try not to hate you. Even when you picked the poison over me. Even when you left me with nothing but pain and rage. I get it now. The world's got a way of chewing people up and spitting them out. And you were just another meal.

You deserved better. So did I.

But they took you from me, Mom. Beat you down and left you to rot like you were nothing. And now I'm here—

I'm here, dragging your ghost with me like some disease. I'm here, shouting your name into the dark even though I know you can't hear me. I'm here, trying to swallow this hate that keeps growing.

I tell myself you're at peace now. That the poison can't hurt you anymore. But I'm still here. Still drowning.

The only way I'll find peace is by making them pay.

For you. For me.

Some days, I hear your voice. Not the slurred, angry version. But the real one, from before everything went to hell. Then it's gone, and

all I remember is your body — cold
and twisted, left to rot like you
never mattered.

The world failed you. I failed you.
And that heaviness is chained to
me, dragging me down.

But maybe you're free now.
Somewhere the hunger can't reach
you. Somewhere your laughter
doesn't sound like breaking glass.

I want to believe you're okay.
That you got away from
everything that ruined you. But I
couldn't save you. So I'll settle for
revenge.

Because that's all I have left.

I folded the paper and shoved it deep into my
pocket. It wasn't just a letter. It was a confession,
a curse, and a promise. A vow scrawled in pain.
One I intended to keep. I carried everywhere I
went. It felt like trying to bury a part of me that
refused to heal. The closest thing I'll have to a
funeral. But writing it down hadn't helped. It

only made the rage sharper, the appetite worse.

The city didn't care about my grief. It just kept breathing, pulsing with its own sickness. It wasn't just me; it was everyone. I heard it whispered in alleyways and murmured around burn barrels — stories of brothers, sisters, mothers, and fathers left dead without a second thought. "Cops don't come for us," an old man told me once, his voice crackling with age and despair. "Not unless we spill out into their pretty streets or start shooting where the rich folks live." A woman nodded beside him; her hands wrapped tight around a chipped coffee mug. "They don't even look into it. Just another dead junkie. Just another body." Their words coiled around my heart like barbed wire, binding me tighter to my purpose. I learned to survive by becoming just as hard and cold as the world around me

The world had become nothing but restless nights and endless searching. Days melted into weeks, weeks stretched into months, and the appetite only grew. It was all I had. My purpose. My religion.

I'd been drifting since she died. Bouncing between homes and shelters like a leaf caught in a storm. No one noticed the boy who never stayed long. No one asked questions. If I kept my head down, my stomach full, and my feet moving, I could pass through the fractures without anyone caring where I came from or where I was going.

Shelters were hellish places. Rooms crammed with desperate souls clawing for scraps of kindness. I remember Clarence—a man missing three fingers on his left hand, chopped off by some dealer for stealing. He'd sit by the fire barrel, hands curled like claws, voice like gravel. "You think you're gonna make it out of here, kid?" he'd ask, voice cracking with the cold. I never answered. He'd laugh, a ragged sound. "You won't," he'd say, shaking his head. "Not unless you got something to fight for. Otherwise, you're just another ghost wandering these alleys." He'd tap his three fingers against the barrel, the sound hollow and sharp. "You take from this city, it takes back. Always does."

I learned quickly to sleep with one eye open, to hide what little I had, and never trust a hand

extended in friendship. Theft, violence, abuse —
these were constants, just as much as hunger and
the cold.

I spent nights curled up beneath stairwells,
wrapped in newspapers that crinkled like dry
leaves. I scavenged food from dumpsters behind
diners and scoured the gutters for loose change.
The city was brutal, but it taught me how to
survive.

Survival was everything. Survival meant I could
keep searching.

The name came to me like a whispered curse,
carried on by the voices of addicts and dealers
who lurked in the shadows. King Kobb. His name
hung heavy in the air, spoken with fear and
reverence. He ruled corners from Kensington to
Frankford, peddling poison to the desperate.

I pieced the truth together like fragments of a
shattered mirror—jagged and gleaming with the
light of things better left unseen. King Kobb's
name was etched into the marrow of the city,
whispered in back alleys where the walls seemed
to listen and scrawled in the margins of

whispered fears. His name lingered like the bitter taste of iron on your tongue—sharp, metallic, and impossible to forget.

They said his throne was built from the spoils of desperation, an empire stretching across fractured streets and boarded-up windows, where graffiti curled and twisted like angry vines clawing at the concrete. His kingdom sprawled through crumbling buildings and rust-streaked fire escapes, each block a jagged tooth in the city's grin.

Police cruisers loitered at the corners, engines idling with a low, mechanical hum. Officers leaned back in their seats, eyes glazed and unblinking, watching figures drift through alleyways like marionettes, pulled along by invisible strings. A flicker of movement. The glow of a cigarette. Deals exchanged with hands that moved quick and silent, practiced in their precision.

To them, this place wasn't a city—it was a mausoleum still waiting for its dead. A kingdom suspended in limbo, where survival was the only currency and the crown belonged to the one whose hands were the heaviest with sin.

He reigned over it like a phantom conductor, unseen but everywhere. They said he wore the city's chaos like a mantle, his footsteps silent, his gaze cold and unyielding. And when he came for you, it wasn't a reckoning. It was just the city collecting its debt.

I'd decided he was the one. The monster who beat my mother to death and left her to rot. Maybe it wasn't him. Maybe it was someone just like him. But it didn't matter. They were all the same. Dealers. Parasites. Predators that fed on suffering. Killing him would be justice—a cleansing of the filth that stained the streets.

But before I could hunt, I had to be ready. My life had become what my mother always feared—a child abandoned to the city's open jaws, swallowed by concrete and vice. School became a distant echo. I stopped going altogether. The teachers stopped asking questions. I was just another name crossed off the roll call, another kid chewed up by the system, spat out into the gutters where hope went to die.

David tried to pull me back, his concern a lifeline I kept severing, thread by thread, until it was nothing but frayed whispers. But he never stopped. Every day, he would find me—somehow, some way—his eyes searching mine for remnants of the person I used to be, like he was sifting through ashes for a spark that hadn't yet burned out.

"Derrick, man, what are you doing?" he'd ask, voice tight with something raw and aching. "You're missing everything. They got you marked as a dropout now. You gonna throw it all away?" His words cracked, splintered by the weight of his desperation. He held onto hope like it was slipping through his fingers, gripping tight even as it unraveled strand by strand.

I shrugged him off, my eyes fixed on the cracked pavement, the broken bottles glimmering like dead stars in the gutter. "I got stuff to do," I'd say, my voice hollow.

He sighed, heavy and long, like he was breathing in the weight I carried. "You think this is living?"

he asked me once, voice barely above a whisper. "This ain't living, man. This is just waiting to die."

I didn't answer. I couldn't risk him getting caught in the fire. He didn't deserve the version of me I was becoming.

One day, he blocked my path, his body rigid with resolve. "You think you're doing something?" His voice was raw, edged with something I didn't want to name—hope. "This ain't you, man. This ain't how it's supposed to be."

I wouldn't look at him. "You don't know what it's supposed to be."

"I know it's not this!" His hand came down on my shoulder, firm but trembling. "You don't have to disappear. We can fix it. Whatever it is."

I jerked away, the movement sharp enough to sting. "Ain't nothing to fix."

David stared at me, his hand still hovering in the air like he was trying to catch something that was already gone. His eyes softened, the fight draining from his shoulders. "I don't recognize you," he whispered.

"Good," I said, turning my back on him. "You ain't supposed to." I couldn't explain the rage.

I didn't feel I needed to.

Time collapsed into itself—days blurred into weeks, each one darker and sharper than the last. Survival became ritual. I stole when desperation bit too deep. I learned to fight, to hide, to endure. The city was a predator, and I was its restless prey.

But every night, I thought of him. King Kobb. His name hung heavy around my neck, a chain I couldn't break. I listened to addicts ramble, to dealers boast in darkened alleys. His name moved like a whisper, infecting every corner, every block. The man who would be my reckoning.

But wanting him dead wasn't enough. I needed a plan.

I spent days trailing the men who worked for him. Watching the deals go down, learning their routines. Faces and names became familiar. Their patterns etched into my memory.

But I was still just a boy. And boys didn't kill men like King Kobb.

I needed something more. Something that would make him fear me.

A gun.

Finding one was harder than I thought. Weeks turned into months, my desperation festering like a wound. I searched every corner I knew—crack dens with their flickering lights, abandoned houses crumbling from the inside out, and the rusted husks of cars where ghosts of the forgotten huddled to burn their poisons. I whispered my questions in alleys thick with depression, slipped wrinkled bills into cracked hands, but still, nothing. Guns weren't easy to come by, not if you were just a kid with nothing but rage and vengeance in your pockets.

Finally, I got a name: "Old Man Harris." He was a veteran, they said. Lived under the overpass, buried deep in the city's bones like a splinter that wouldn't heal. People whispered he had a stash—guns, ammo, relics of a war he couldn't shake. Some said he traded them for favors; others said he'd swap them just to hear a good story.

I found him hunched over a shopping cart beneath the overpass, its wheels crooked and squealing with each nudge. His eyes were glassy but sharp, cutting through the fog of madness like shards of broken glass. A cigarette dangled from his lips, the ash stretching dangerously long before crumbling to the ground.

He saw me coming. "You got business, or you just gonna stare?" he rasped, the cigarette bobbing with each word.

"I need a gun," I said, voice steady even though my insides were churning.

He laughed—a gravelly, broken sound that rattled in his chest. "You ain't got the heart for it, kid."

I stepped closer, the smell of mildew and stale smoke clawing at my throat. "I got the heart," I replied, my voice colder than I expected. "I just don't got the gun."

He studied me for a moment, eyes flicking over my frame like he was assessing damage. "What you plan to do with it?"

"Handle some business," I said.

Harris grinned, revealing a smile where teeth used to be. "Business, huh? You look more like trouble than business." He reached into the heap of junk in his cart and pulled out a flask, taking a long swig before wiping his mouth with the back of his hand. "Guns ain't cheap. And they ain't free."

"I got money," I lied, reaching into my pocket and flashing him a handful of determined bills. It was everything I had, barely enough to buy a hot meal, but I held it out like it was a fortune.

He glanced at the cash, then back at me. "That ain't even half," he muttered, shaking his head. "But...maybe we can work something out."

My pulse quickened. "What do you need?"

His eyes hardened. "A story," he said, leaning back against the concrete wall, the cigarette smoldering between his fingers. "Not just any story. I want the truth. Why's a kid like you need a gun?"

The words spilled out before I could stop them—rage, grief, vengeance all wrapped up in a knot too tight to untangle. I told him about her. About the man who killed her. About Christmas Eve and the silence that followed. Harris listened, unmoving, his eyes never leaving mine.

When I finished, he crushed the cigarette beneath his boot. "Damn," he whispered, almost reverently. "Ain't that somethin'." He reached back into the cart, rummaging through blankets and cans until he pulled out a pistol wrapped in an old flannel shirt. "Colt .38," he said, turning it over in his hands like it was sacred. "Ain't much, but it'll do the job."

He held it out, and I stepped forward, hands steady this time. My fingers wrapped around the cold metal, and for the first time, it felt real. Heavy. Dangerous.

Harris's eyes softened, just a little. "You remember one thing," he said, his voice gravelly but solemn. "It don't get easier. Only deeper."

I nodded, slipping the gun into my waistband, feeling the weight of it settle against my hip. "I'm counting on it," I replied, turning away before he could see the flicker of something like fear dance across my face.

As I walked back into the city's shadows, I heard his voice echo off the concrete. "Hope you find what you're looking for, kid. Hope it's worth it."

I didn't look back. I walked until I found a patch of darkness where the world forgot to look, and there, I pulled it from my waistband.

The gun settled into my hand—heavy and uneven, its barrel flecked with rust, the grip cracked and worn from years of use. It felt like holding a secret, something cold and unyielding, built for consequence. But it was mine now. A tool. A weapon. Something that could take life from a distance, untouched by the warmth of blood or the feeling of flesh giving way. It was power—clean, efficient, and absolute. Death delivered with a single pull of the trigger.

But it was more than that. It was control. It was choice. In a world that had stolen everything from me, this was something I could take back. I could decide who walked away and who didn't. I could decide who mattered and who vanished.

In that moment, I understood—it wasn't just the weapon I needed. It was the feeling. The certainty. The sense that, for once, I held the cards. I would need more of that. More control. More moments where the world bowed to my will instead of the other way around.

My fingers traced the rough edges of the grip, feeling each groove, each imperfection like they were lines on a map. I whispered to it, my voice low and reverent, as if it could hear me. "You're different," I murmured, my breath ghosting over the barrel. "You're power. You're silence." The words spilled from my lips unbidden, more prayer than thought.

I tightened my grip, feeling it mold to my hand like it belonged there, heavy and righteous. "You don't need blood on your hands," I whispered, eyes locked on the iron sight. "Just a pull. Just a whisper."

In that moment, the gun was a promise—an unspoken vow etched in steel and rust.

The blade was personal; this was something else entirely—an extension of my will. And I wasn't afraid of it. I craved it. It didn't breathe like the knife did. It didn't need to feel flesh split or watch blood spill out slow. It was distant, clinical. A whisper turned into thunder. I turned it over in my hands, studying its lines, feeling its weight. The knife was an intimacy in violence. This... this was a reckoning.

I tested it on rats first, their bodies twitching and stilling with each shot. It made the appetite quiet, if only for a moment. The trigger's click still echoed in my bones, a vibration I couldn't shake. My fingers flexed around the grip, feeling the solid weight of it—an extension of my own hand. I didn't just feel powerful. I was powerful. For the first time, the city didn't feel bigger than me. For the first time, I wasn't prey. I was something else entirely.

I needed that power.

I spent weeks tracking his men, moving like a shadow through the city's grime. I studied them from a distance, learning their routines, their habits. They were soldiers with predictable patterns. Men who took orders without question and scattered like cockroaches when Kobb barked.

The dealers pushed poison from street corners and darkened doorways. I watched them trade money for misery, their faces hollow and eyes clouded by greed or fear. Sometimes I'd catch a name or a whisper, something I could use.

But it was never enough. Just fragments. Pieces of a puzzle that never fit together. And every time I thought I was getting close, he would slip away.

I knew I couldn't face him in his fortress, surrounded by his dogs. I needed to catch him alone. Vulnerable.

Then, one night, I got lucky.

It was raining, the city's filth washing into gutters like blood rinsed from a wound. I followed one of his men, a thick-necked thug named Benny, who always trailed a few steps behind Kobb like a leashed animal.

They met in a cramped bar off Lehigh Avenue,

the kind of place where the air tasted like sweat and old booze. Benny kept watch near the door, but Kobb wandered to the back alone. Drunk. Careless.

I waited until Kobb stumbled out, his laughter slurred, his body swaying like he was held up by threads that had started to fray. Benny had drifted into conversation with some woman, his attention swallowed whole.

The alley stretched long and narrow, choked with the smell of rot and rain-soaked brick. Old newspapers clung to the pavement, their edges curling like dead leaves. Rusted fire escapes loomed above, dripping with water that slapped the concrete in slow, steady rhythms. He moved through it like he owned the space, shoulders squared, coat flaring with each staggered step. His boots splashed through puddles rimmed with oil and ash, the filth leaping up to stain the cuffs of his pants.

I followed, my footsteps swallowed by the rain, steady and unhurried. He didn't look back—why would he? Men like Kobb never expected retribution to walk right up to their doorstep. Not from someone like me.

Her memory clung to the walls of that alley. I saw her in the streaks of rain running down the brick, her laugh caught in the splatter of water pooling in cracked asphalt. She used to hold my hand back when I believed in things like love. Her hands were soft then, unmarked by the needle's cruel kiss. We'll get out of here, she'd say, her eyes bright with dreams too fragile to survive.

But we never did. She never did. And it was because of him.

He stopped beneath a flickering streetlamp, the bulb humming with the threat of collapse. He fumbled with his lighter, the tiny flame spitting and snapping before it finally caught. It lit his face in sharp relief—deep lines etched with greed, eyes soulless and washed out. He brought the cigarette to his lips, inhaled, and exhaled a cloud of smoke that drifted into the rain and vanished.

I kept walking, closing the distance one step at a time. My hands stayed loose at my sides, fingers curling and uncurling with each breath. I didn't reach for anything. I didn't need to.

"Kid." His voice broke the silence, rough and ragged. He didn't turn around. "You been followin' me for three blocks. That's either real brave or real stupid. Which one is it?"

I stopped just shy of the light's reach, the rain dripping from my jacket, pooling around my feet. I watched him, the slow tilt of his head as he finally turned to look at me. His eyes raked over my face, searching for recognition. He didn't find it.

"You looking for a job?" he asked, flicking ash from his cigarette, the embers sparking as they hit the wet ground. "Or you got a death wish?"

I didn't answer. Didn't blink. The rain ran down my face, sliding past my lips. His eyes narrowed.

"What, cat got your tongue?" He sneered, baring stained teeth. "You got business with me? 'Cause if you do, I don't like it when people waste my time."

I stepped forward, just enough to be seen. "You don't remember me."

His face faltered, just for a second. He squinted, took another drag of his cigarette. "Should I?"

"You should."

He chuckled, shaking his head. "I meet a lot of people, kid. I don't got time to remember every stray that crosses my path." He dropped the cigarette to the pavement, grinding it under his heel. "But you clearly got somethin' to say." He spread his arms wide, palms up. "So go on, get it off your chest."

I didn't move. Didn't flinch. Just let him stand there, hands open like he was holding court. His grin slipped, just a little.

"What, you think you're gonna spook me with the silent routine?" He scoffed, stuffing his hands into his coat pockets. "You're barkin' up the wrong tree, kid. I've seen worse than you on a bad day."

I took another step forward, slow and deliberate. His hands flexed in his pockets. His shoulders tightened. I saw it—the twitch of his fingers, the way his eyes flickered to the mouth of the alley, calculating the distance, the escape routes. He wasn't sure anymore. He couldn't read me.

"What's your problem, huh?" He spat the words out, gravel in his voice. "You got somethin' to say, say it. Or turn your little ass around and walk back the way you came."

But I didn't turn around. I didn't move. I just stood there, rain pooling around my feet, eyes locked on his. He shifted again, weight rocking from one foot to the other. I watched his hand twitch inside his coat, fingers brushing the edge of something heavy.

"You don't remember me," I said, voice low and flat.

His jaw clenched. "You got about five seconds to say your piece, kid." His hand slipped further into his coat. I watched the fabric bunch around the bulge of a pistol, the outline barely visible through the damp wool. He was daring me to flinch, daring me to make the first move.

But I didn't. I just stared him down, unblinking, watching as the confidence leaked from his eyes drop by drop. The hand inside his coat shook—just a little, just enough for me to see it. His breathing picked up, nostrils flaring. He swallowed, hard, the bob of his throat slick with rain.

"Who the hell are you?" His voice cracked, the sound sharper than the crackle of rain against the metal dumpster behind him.

I took another step forward. He took one back. The distance shrank, and with it, his composure. His eyes darted left and right, searching the alley for any sign of life. Nothing. No Benny. No backup. Just him, me, and the wet stink of decay.

"You don't get it," I said, my voice slipping between us like a blade. "You're already dead. I'm just here to watch you realize it."

His mouth opened, a whisper of breath escaping before he caught it. His fingers curled tight around the grip of his pistol, knuckles whitening beneath the fabric. He didn't draw it. He didn't dare. I saw the hesitation, the fear threading through his bravado, cracking it wide open. For the first time, Kobb was afraid.

"You know who I am?" I asked, stepping closer. The rain slipped down my face, dripping from my chin, pooling around my feet. He swallowed hard, gaze flicking back to his pistol, then to me. He didn't answer. So I asked again. "Do you even remember her?"

His brow furrowed, eyes narrowing. "Who?" His voice cracked on the word. He tried to hide it with a cough.

I felt the burn rise up my throat, like bile. "You beat her to death. Christmas Eve. She owed you money. You remember now?"

His eyes flashed with something—recognition, maybe. His hand twitched around the pistol, and for a second, I thought he might actually pull it. But he just stood there, rain pooling in the creases of his jacket, staring at me with that same sneer I remembered. "I kill a lot of people, kid. You think I remember some junkie?" He laughed, short and sharp. "She shoulda paid up."

My vision swam. I took another step forward, the alley growing smaller, the world shrinking to just us. "She was my mother."

The words hung in the air, heavy and unforgiving. He blinked, and for a moment—just a moment—there was something like regret in his eyes. But it passed, and his mouth curled up into a grin. "Then I guess she shoulda thought about you before she decided to fuck me over."

Something inside me snapped. I didn't even feel my hand move. My finger squeezed the trigger, and the shot shattered the silence. His eyes went wide, disbelief tangled with agony as he staggered backward, clutching at his chest. His mouth opened, but no words came—just a wet, gurgling sound that spilled into the rain. He looked at me like he wanted to ask why, like he thought there was still time for answers. But I had none to give him.

He collapsed, the weight of him slapping the pavement, water splashing up from the force. I watched him writhe, fingers clawing at nothing, until finally, his body went still. The rain kept falling, washing the blood from the cracks in the concrete, carrying it away like it never mattered.

I stepped forward and stared down at him. The

rain pooled around his body, seeping into the fabric of his coat. His eyes were still open, glassy and wide, fixed on nothing. I wondered if he saw her in those last moments—if her face was the last thing burned into his mind. I hoped it was.

I waited for something—regret, fear, even the flicker of doubt. But it didn't come. There was only the sound of rain against pavement and the hum of distant traffic. I breathed in, and the weight that had been pressing on my chest for years was gone. It was like stepping into clean air after being buried alive.

I left him there, drowning in the wet stink of his own decisions, hands still curled like claws, eyes still wide, alone in the alley with nothing but ghosts and regrets.

The city moved on as if nothing happened. Traffic hummed, footsteps shuffled, addicts slipped back into their familiar corners like ghosts haunting their own decay. Life continued its indifferent march, and I wanted to scream at them—shake their shoulders, force them to remember.

"You hear about the dealer that got dropped?" I

asked a man loitering by the corner, his eyes glazed and hollow. He shrugged, flicking ash from his cigarette.

"Which one? Ain't nobody gonna miss 'em. They're like roaches—more just crawl out the cracks."

His indifference stung more than the recoil. "Nobody cares," he muttered, shaking his head. "Dead dealer's just another empty spot on the corner."

I scoured the news, scanned the papers—nothing. Kobb's name was a whisper in the wind, gone before it even touched the lips of those who knew him. A dead dealer wasn't worth ink or airtime. I understood then: if I wanted them to remember, it had to be bigger. Louder. His name couldn't just disappear; it had to be carved into their memory. One dead man was a ripple. I needed to be the wave.

Two days later, I found myself back at the alley, pulled there by something I couldn't name. The rain had come and gone, rinsing away the blood and pooling in the cracks like ghosts lingering in shallow graves. I half expected yellow tape, chalk outlines, flashing lights—but there was nothing. Just concrete stained dark, littered with cigarette butts and discarded bottles.

A woman walked by, her scarf pulled tight against the chill. She glanced at the spot where Kobb had fallen, shaking her head. "Another dead dealer, probably," she muttered to the man beside her. "Ain't nobody care. Just another body in the gutter."

He grunted, flicking his cigarette to the ground. "Nobody comes around for that. Not unless it's a big hit or some white kid gets caught in the crossfire."

Their voices drifted off, swallowed by the city's hum. I stood there, alone, the truth hardening in my bones like concrete: the city devoured its own. And no one came looking.

I could almost hear her voice—soft, reverent, like the words were sacred. "For the Lord loves justice and does not forsake his faithful ones. They are preserved forever, but the children of the wicked shall be cut off." Her favorite verse. She'd recite it on the good days, when the poison hadn't yet hollowed her out. I remembered the way her eyes lit up with belief, like justice wasn't just a word, but a promise.

"The children of the wicked shall be cut off," I whispered under my breath, the words slipping between my teeth like glass shards. "Cut off."

The morning sun broke through the clouds, turning the sky a dull gray, as if the city itself couldn't decide between dawn and dusk. I wandered the streets without direction, the weight of the gun like a promise in my pocket. Its heft was more than just steel—it was purpose. Kobb was dead, and nobody cared. No sirens. No tape. No headlines. Just rain-slicked concrete washing away his blood like it was never there.

The city had swallowed him whole, just like it did with my mother. Like it did with all of us. It was then I understood—there would be no justice for people like her. No one would come searching. No one would pay. Only I could make it right. I had to be the reckoning. If the city wouldn't remember, I would force it to.

Kobb was dead. I had done it. But the satisfaction I'd expected to feel was nothing more than a distant echo. I could almost hear her whisper, faint and hollow, threading through the cracks of memory. "You did good, baby. You did good." It was her voice before the poison had eaten it away—soft, warm, filled with pride I had long since forgotten.

For a moment, I held onto it, let it settle into the hollow spaces Kobb left behind. But like everything else, it faded. A phantom of peace that never really existed. I kept walking, the city blurring around me, the air thick and unwelcoming. It was like walking through ash, each step stirring up the remnants of lives long forgotten.

My feet led me through parts of the city that seemed forgotten even by time. The streets twisted into each other, knotted and overgrown, marked by crumbling bricks and windows sealed with molded boards. They stared back like doll's eyes, shattered glass glinting in the dim light. Sidewalks cracked open under the weight of neglect, weeds forcing their way through the gaps, trash piling high in the gutters like crude memorials.

Faces loomed from the alleys—gaunt addicts with vacant stares, kids too young to be so hardened, their expressions carved from loss and survival. Rusted cars sat abandoned, stripped down to their bones, the remnants of upholstery spilling out like entrails. The city wasn't just a backdrop— it was something alive, feeding on those who couldn't fight back. It swallowed the weak, buried the forgotten, and wore their remnants like trophies. I walked through its belly, just another ghost, unseen and unmissed.

My thoughts tangled around themselves, fevered and restless. Everything felt warped, like I'd wandered too far from anything that made sense. Kobb's death played on a loop in my head—his blood spreading like ink, pooling into the cracks as his life seeped out. It didn't feel like I'd been the one to pull the trigger. More like I'd watched someone else do it, my body just a vessel for the rage.

I can still remember the numbness that followed,

it was worse than the fury. Anger, at least, had weight—it pushed me forward, made me feel human. Now, all I had was emptiness, dragging me down like stones tied to my ankles. The silence wrapped around me, clinging and suffocating. I started seeing things that weren't there—flickers at the edges of my vision, shapes shifting in the corners of the alleys. I spun around, chest tight, but there was nothing—just abandoned streets and crumbling facades staring back at me.

The whispers came next—threads of sound woven into the hum of the city, too faint to make out, too persistent to ignore. I'd jerk my head toward the source, heart pounding, only to find cracked concrete and flickering streetlights. I knew it wasn't real. It couldn't be. But the whispers didn't stop, dragging me deeper into the maze, calling me to listen, to follow. It felt like the city was breathing—exhaling secrets only I could hear. Or maybe I was just losing myself, sinking into the language of the streets.

People passed by without looking—blurred faces wrapped up in their own struggles, eyes sliding over me like I was nothing more than a smudge on their day. Some glanced sideways, like they could sense something off, like they could smell the violence lingering on my skin. Or maybe it was paranoia. Maybe the sickness was mine alone.

I kept moving, wandering through the haze, unsure if I was looking for a way out or just waiting for something to catch up. That's when the police car pulled up alongside me, headlights slicing through the mist. The window slid down, and the officer leaned out, his gaze sharp, dissecting.

"You out here alone, kid?" His tone was casual, but his eyes probed, testing.

I nodded, hands deep in my pockets. "Where you heading?" he asked, not looking away.

"Nowhere," I said, flat and detached.

He glanced at his partner, who gave a small shrug. "Nowhere's a long walk," the partner chimed in.

"I got time," I replied, voice steady.

The older cop's eyes narrowed, studying me. "Got a name?"

"Yeah," I said, unblinking. "But it's mine."

He smirked without warmth. "Smart mouth. You got folks looking for you?"

"Not anymore."

He paused, nodding slowly, like he'd heard it all before. "Yeah. That's how it goes, huh?"

Silence stretched out, thick and buzzing. Finally, he leaned back in his seat, still watching me. "Stay out of trouble," he said, his tone softening just a bit.

"Or don't," his partner added, voice flat. "Your choice."

The window slid back up, and the car pulled away, tires hissing against the wet pavement. I stood there, the gun pressing against my ribs, pulse hammering in my throat. I couldn't shake the feeling they saw more than they let on—that maybe my name was already circulating through the precinct, tied to something brutal and unforgivable.

I watched the taillights disappear into the fog, breath slipping out in ragged bursts. I turned back to the street, ready to disappear again, but then I heard it—the low rumble of an engine reversing, creeping back through the mist.

The cruiser returned, taillights slicing back through the rain, the wipers smearing water from the windshield. My heart dropped into my stomach.

The window slid down again, slower this time, the older cop leaning out, his eyes sharper now, more alert. "Hey, kid. Hold up a second."

My hands tightened in my pockets, fingertips brushing against cold metal. I swallowed hard. "Something wrong?" I asked, my voice slipping out rough, uneven.

He reached into the dashboard and pulled out a folded piece of paper, smoothing it against his knee before holding it up. "You look real familiar," he said, turning the paper so I could see. "This you?"

My breath caught. It was me—but not like this. I

was smaller, softer around the edges. My hair was combed, neat, a button-down shirt snug against my frame. A Sunday suit. The photo was creased and grainy, but the eyes were the same.

The officer's gaze flickered back to me, studying my reaction. "What, you forget you clean up good?"

I couldn't answer. My tongue felt heavy, my throat tight. I remembered that suit—scratchy and stiff, the collar pressing against my neck. My mother had straightened the lapels, spit-shined my shoes right before we walked into church. Her hands had been steady then, not shaking like they did near the end. She'd called me handsome, kissed my forehead, told me I'd make her proud.

"You got family looking for you," the cop continued, his voice softer now, almost gentle. "They've been searching for a while." He paused, eyes locked on mine. "Your grandparents."

I blinked, the rain falling heavier now, streaking down my face. "My grandparents?"

The officer nodded, leaning back a bit, the tension

in his shoulders unwinding. "They've been looking since you disappeared. Had this picture sent out with some flyers a while back." He tapped the photo. "Guess you slipped through the cracks."

I swallowed hard, the memories uncoiling from places I'd buried them. I remembered soft voices, hands that never shook, dinners that didn't come out of cans. I remembered safety, warmth that didn't need to be earned.

The partner leaned over, his eyes softer now. "They want you back, kid. Come on, let's get you off the street."

I stared at the photo one last time, then back at them. The city still whispered behind me, tugging at my edges. But this…this was real.

I took a step forward, then another. The car door popped open, and I climbed inside.

They took me to my grandparents' house in Frankford. A place that felt like a different world. The air was clean, untouched by the hate and tension that had clung to my skin for as long as I could remember. Polished wood floors gleamed beneath my feet, smooth and unblemished, not like the warped and water-stained boards I was used to. The walls were painted soft shades of cream and pale blue, and sunlight actually seeped through the windows instead of flickering through torn blinds. It smelled of lavender and lemon polish, of dinners cooked at regular times and laundry folded neatly in wicker baskets. It smelled like order. Like rules.

My grandparents asked questions, their voices soft and careful, as if their words might break me if spoken too loudly. My grandmother's hands fluttered around me, smoothing my collar, brushing imaginary dust from my shoulders, the way you would tend to a fragile heirloom. Her touch was light, barely there, as if afraid I might shatter beneath her fingertips. My grandfather watched from the doorway, his hands clasped in front of him, shoulders squared but eyes tired. He nodded at everything I said, as if agreement alone could keep me from unraveling.

I gave them the answers they needed. Lies wrapped carefully in truth. I'd gotten good at that. I told them I was fine. That I was ready to start over. That I was just happy to be somewhere safe. I watched the relief spill over their faces, the way they glanced at each other with silent gratitude, like my words had cleansed me of everything I'd seen. I let them believe it. I let them think I'd left it all behind.

They told me they'd collected Mom's ashes. They wanted to hold a proper funeral. My grandfather's voice cracked when he spoke of it, eyes glimmering with a grief he tried to swallow. "She always said she wanted to come back here... raise you right," he murmured, voice trembling. My grandmother squeezed his hand, her eyes wet and distant. I nodded, offering words they needed to hear, pretending that the memories of her still lived somewhere in me.

But I couldn't tell them the truth—about the emptiness inside or how taking vengeance had only deepened the hollow space left behind.

They thought they were saving me.

As I sat in that warm, tidy room filled with memories I couldn't connect to, I knew this was just another place to hide. A temporary illusion of safety until the emptiness called to me again. I'd come home, but home was now something forever out of reach.

But the truth hung heavy around me: I was already beyond saving.

Psalm 88:18 whispered through my mind like an old, familiar curse. "You have taken from me friend and neighbor—darkness is my closest friend."

I stared at the photographs along the walls, familiar faces smiling from behind glass. Yet all I felt was the pressing weight of everything I couldn't say, everything I'd hidden away.

I was back in a place that called itself home. But I was more alone now than ever before.

The house was too quiet.

Their house was nothing like the places I'd slept before. It smelled of lavender and something sweet, like fresh bread left to cool on the counter. The floors were polished wood, gleaming in the dull morning light. Every room held a feeling I couldn't touch.

They tried. I could tell. Their voices were careful, soft as if volume alone could shatter me. My grandmother would hover, eyes filled with worry and love she didn't know how to give. My grandfather kept his distance, his concern masked by gruff attempts at conversation that always ended too quickly.

"Got everything you need, Derrick?" he'd ask, arms crossed like he was bracing for bad news.

I'd nod, the lies slipping out with ease. "Yeah. I'm good."

Good. The word felt like a foreign language. I couldn't remember the last time it applied to me.

They tried to pull me into their routines—meals at the table, conversations about school I hadn't attended in months. I played along, giving them what they needed to hear.

But every night, when the house finally fell silent, I felt the blackness close in. I'd lie awake, staring at the ceiling until it faded into shadows. My mind wandered back to the streets, to the echo of gunshots, to the blood staining my hands.

Looking back at his death. I'd gotten my revenge. But the hunger remained, gnawing at me from the inside. Killing him hadn't fixed anything. It only made the emptiness deeper. I realize now that vengeance didn't satisfy the hunger, it barely felt justified.

I spent my days wandering the neighborhood, avoiding their watchful eyes. Frankford was different from the corners I'd come from. It was quieter, the violence tucked away beneath neatly trimmed lawns and houses painted with care.

But even here, the darkness followed me. Lurking at the edges of every thought, whispering that I didn't belong.

One afternoon, my grandfather caught me staring at the framed photographs lining the hallway.

"That's your mother," he said, his voice rough but gentle. "Back when she was a kid. Before everything went wrong."

I stared at the photo, my mother's face frozen in a smile I'd never seen. She looked so...happy. Like someone else entirely.

"She used to love this place," my grandfather continued. "Always said she'd come back and raise you here. Make things right."

"She never made it," I replied, my voice flat.

"No," he admitted, eyes clouded by regret. "But that doesn't mean you can't."

I couldn't meet his gaze. The burden of his hope was too powerful. I mumbled something about needing air and walked out the front door before he could stop me.

I roamed the streets for hours, my feet carrying me to places that felt familiar in their deterioration. I wanted the noise, the chaos, anything to drown out the quiet that followed me everywhere.

But nothing worked. Not the noise. Not the wandering. The emptiness stayed with me, feeding on every attempt to fill it.

By the time I made it back to my grandparents' house, the sky was dark, and their worry was painted across their faces.

"We were starting to think you weren't coming back," my grandmother said, her voice trembling.

"I always come back."

It was a lie. Because part of me never did.

Later that night, I lay awake in the bed they'd made up for me. It smelled clean—too clean. Like it belonged to someone who hadn't been swallowed by the streets. Everything felt sharp-edged and unnatural.

Their kindness was genuine. My grandmother had prepared dinner, the warmth of the food a distant memory I could hardly remember tasting. My grandfather asked questions, his words careful like he was trying not to shatter something delicate.

They wanted to help me, but they couldn't reach the part of me that mattered. Couldn't touch the hollowness I carried. They tried, though. Offered comfort like blankets to a freezing man who couldn't feel the warmth.

I heard them talking late that night. Their voices muffled through the thin walls, laced with concern and desperation.

"He barely eats," my grandmother whispered, her words thick with fear. "He's so thin, so...lost."

"He just needs time," my grandfather replied. "We have to be patient. Give him space."

I shut my eyes tighter, their voices threading into my thoughts like needles. They were trying to pull me back, but I was already too far gone.

The darkness was all I had left. It was familiar. It was mine.

As I drifted into sleep, wrapped in warmth I couldn't feel, I knew the truth no one else would say: I was already lost. And no one saves the damned.

THOU SHALT KILL WITH PURPOSE

August 1985

Poem - Baptism of Blade

By fire's kiss and steel's embrace,
I tread where shadows leave no
trace.
Through blood-drenched streets
where angels weep,
I cull the tainted from their sleep.

Their sins entwined with filth and
grief,
A festering wound with no relief.

Yet through the blade, redemption
breeds,
A beautiful mercy born of deeds.

Where light recoils from what I
am,
A harvester where none dare
stand.
For purity's edge, so cold and
keen,
Cuts deeper than what eyes have
seen.

It had been nearly two years since I last fed the hunger. Two years of trying to drown it beneath scripture and sermons, beneath the forced smiles of the congregation and my grandparents' strained hope. I tried to forget the satisfaction that came with the kill—the stillness it had brought, if only for a moment. I tried to convince myself that I could live a normal life, that the darkness within me could be starved into submission. But that was just the kind of lie you tell yourself when the truth is too sharp to swallow. The hunger never left. It only slept, coiled tight and patient.

Goldie's made that impossible.

The bar hunched on the corner like it had grown

there, brick by brick, from the rot of the neighborhood. Its sickness didn't just bleed into the pavement; it sank in, soaking into the cracks like poison, staining everything it touched. By night, it became a breeding ground for the city's new plague—a poison that burned hotter and faster than anything before it. They called it *crack*, and it spread like wildfire, eating its way through the streets, hollowing people out until they were nothing but husks of who they used to be. Goldie's was the heart of that decomposition, a place where dignity withered and desperation fed on itself like a snake devouring its own tail.

It was a monument to every impulse I tried to bury. I walked past its doors with my hands in my pockets, knuckles clenched around the phantom weight of unfinished business. It was never the faces or the stories that pulled me back—it was the feeling. That slow, creeping certainty that something inside still needed to be fed. That what I'd locked away hadn't died; it had only grown quieter, waiting for the right fracture to spill out.

I told myself I'd moved on, that I'd left the blood and silence behind me. But each step past Goldie's felt like scraping open an old wound, the air heavy with unfulfilled promises. It wasn't a calling—it was a reminder. A weight that pressed against my chest, tightening with every glance at its doors. I'd convinced myself I was different now, that I could walk by without feeling the pull. But that feeling never left. It just sank deeper, coiling itself around my spine, waiting.

My grandparents couldn't see the struggle I was fighting. They only saw a boy who went to church, bowed his head during prayers, and nodded politely when spoken to. They didn't understand the urges simmering beneath the surface.

Their house was a monument to order, every surface gleaming with a sterile brilliance, as if scrubbing away imperfections could bleach the soul clean. My grandmother dusted the mantle with religious precision, three times a day without fail, her hands moving in rhythm like she was praying with each swipe. My grandfather polished the floors until they reflected back their idea of perfection—a portrait of virtue framed in polished wood and spotless glass. The scent of pine and lavender lived in the walls, an almost suffocating reminder that anything unclean had no place there.

But outside their doors, Frankford was unraveling. It wasn't just decaying—it was devouring itself, piece by piece. The streets were veins clogged with poison, pulsing with things that couldn't be washed away. Crack had burned through entire blocks, leaving the shells of what once was, sunken and gutted. Violence crept like a shadow that couldn't be outrun. I walked those streets with my hands in my pockets, eyes forward, pretending the world wasn't coming apart at the seams. I tried to be the person my grandparents whispered about in their prayers, as if their faith alone could anchor me to the light.

I spent months tethered to church pews, the wood rough beneath my hands, the sermons droning on about salvation and the cleansing of the soul. My grandparents' hands gripped mine during prayer, their knuckles pressed white, as if their belief could be transferred through touch. Redemption was spoken of like it was something you could catch if you stood still long enough. I bowed my head, let the words wash over me, but they never stuck. Beneath the surface, there was something that wouldn't fade—a hunger, restless and prowling, curling around my thoughts and waiting for the walls to crack.

But the sermons only twisted the craving, feeding

it rather than quelling it. For every verse about forgiveness, I heard the echo of vengeance. For every promise of salvation, I tasted the blood of the wicked. It was as if the scripture itself was inviting me to purge the city's filth, to act as the blade of righteousness.

They spoke of sin as something curable. A sickness that could be cured through faith and repentance. But my sickness wasn't something words could cure. It was something that demanded blood.

Isaiah 1:16-17 echoed in my mind as a taunt rather than a remedy: "Wash and make yourselves clean. Take your evil deeds out of my sight; stop doing wrong. Learn to do right; seek justice. Defend the oppressed. Take up the cause of the fatherless; plead the case of the widow."

The words churned within me, promising a purity that I could only achieve through bloodshed. To cleanse the city of its stench. To rid the streets of the wicked.

A sermon delivered by the twisted voice within me, whispering that righteousness could only be born from ruin.

The thought festered, spreading like cancer beneath my skin. Each day, it grew stronger—its roots sinking deeper into my mind until it became an obsession. An insatiable need.

My attempts to smother it had only made it more ravenous. It festered beneath the sermons and prayers, wrapping around my thoughts like a snake until they were choked of anything but the urge to kill.

I found myself lingering near Goldie's more often. Watching the people drift in and out, tethered to its shadow like it was the only place they belonged. I told myself I was just passing by, just observing—but I knew better. Goldie's wasn't just a bar. It was a sinkhole, swallowing hope and spitting out hollow shells. The walls held the weight of a thousand secrets, their paint peeling back like old scabs, revealing the history of lives unraveled. Goldie's stood defiant, its neon sign flickering like a heartbeat that refused to stop, even though the body around it was already dead. People staggered in and out, dragging their shadows behind them, leaving pieces of themselves in the cracks of the sidewalk like breadcrumbs no one would ever follow.

The women were the worst. Not for what they did, but for what they conjured—ghosts of my mother clawing for a way out. I watched them spill from Goldie's, bodies bent like wilted flowers left too long in the sun. They moved with a kind of surrender, shoulders hunched, limbs unsteady, as if gravity had grown heavier just for them. My mother had died trying to outrun that weight. But these women returned, over and over, pressing their lips to bottles and pipes like they were sipping from holy cups, baptizing themselves in poison. It wasn't despair—it was devotion, a prayer spoken in exhales and ashes. A message to whatever god promised oblivion. I used to wonder if they even knew they were praying to their own graves, or if the smoke just made it easier to forget.

I carried the knife like a secret, its weight grounding me, whispering promises I wasn't ready to confront. I told myself it was just for protection, a precaution for the streets that never showed mercy. But deep down, I knew better. The blade wasn't just metal and edge—it was a calling, a reminder that control could be taken back with the flick of a wrist.

It was that same illusion of control I searched for in the church pews, squeezed between my grandparents every Sunday morning. I remember those sermons, the way the pastor's voice would rise and fall, weaving tales of redemption and wrath. I remember the smell of old books and polished wood, the fractured sunlight bleeding through stained glass. My grandmother's hands rested gently on her Bible, her fingers brushing the pages as if the words themselves were sacred. But it wasn't the promises of salvation that stayed with me. It was something else. Something I found scrawled in the margins of her Bible—a verse that would change everything. The ink was faded, almost rubbed away, but I could still make it out. *Psalm 101:8.*

"Every morning I will silence all the wicked in the land; I will cut off every evildoer from the city of the Lord."

It hit me differently than the other verses. It didn't sound like comfort or forgiveness or redemption. It sounded like resolve—like a statement of intent. I read it again, the words settling into me like stones dropped into deep water.

Looking back, I realize now why that verse stuck. It wasn't just scripture—it was something more. It didn't feel holy; it felt personal. Almost like a message meant just for me, buried in that old book. It wasn't just an idea; it was direction. A quiet confirmation that maybe the way I saw the world wasn't entirely wrong.

It didn't preach forgiveness or patience. It spoke of cutting out the wicked, of cleansing the land. And that felt right. I couldn't shake the feeling that I'd found something important—a purpose wrapped in holy words. I didn't know it yet, but that verse was already taking root, shaping the way I saw myself.

I continued to watch them stumble from Goldie's, their bodies moving through the night as if they had nowhere to go but nowhere to stay. I watched the way they staggered, like they were tethered to invisible threads, dragged forward by habit and hunger. I imagined what it would be like to sever those threads. To release them from that endless loop of despair. I was only sixteen, but I felt older. Hardened. My childhood buried beneath layers of rage and longing. The craving simmered just beneath my skin, tightening its grip, promising that I could be the hand of righteousness. That the blade wasn't just a weapon—it was an extension of something divine.

For the first time, I didn't shy from the hunger. I believed in it. I believed it was holy.

I would be the instrument of righteousness.

And I would do it my way.

The knife had become a guide, a restless creature pulling me forward. Its thirst twined with mine, urging me to feed it.

I remember the one night, I was walking home, my steps heavy from the heat pressing down on the city like a clenched fist. The streets were emptying out, the sun sinking below the rooftops, shadows stretching long and thick across fractured sidewalks.

I kept my head down, eyes fixed on the pavement. The knife fit my hand like a natural extension, fused to my flesh by purpose. My appetite was too unpredictable now, flaring up without warning, demanding nourishment.

It was the thorn lodged deep within me, digging further each day, its pain both torment and pleasure. A reminder that I had been chosen. Some days it felt like a curse other days a calling.

The lights glowed dim and feverish, drawing me closer like a moth to flame. As if summoned by providence, she emerged from the darkness—an offering cast before me.

She slipped toward me with the gracelessness of a filly just finding its legs, her gait unsteady and foal-like, as if the world itself threatened to swallow her with each uncertain step. Pale skin marred with bruises, her gaze unfocused and wandering. She smelled of cigarettes and regrets. I tried to sidestep her, but she reached for me with fingers that clung like desperation.

"Hey," she slurred. Her voice was distraught, her words slathered together. "You got a smoke? Something to share? You're cute, you know that?"

She laughed, a defeated, joyless sound. Her fingers grazed my arm, nails scratching my skin just enough to sting.

Her touch was profane, a desecration upon my flesh. My chest tightened, breath stuttering as the memory surged up from the depths. The woman who had taken my innocence, leaving me shattered and remade. I saw her in this woman's eyes—empty, dead things gazing through me as if I were nothing but meat.

The anger rose sharp and hot, but I didn't act.

Not yet. But she was marked. Already chosen.

I let her drift away, her words trailing off into the night. I followed her.

The city's decay thickened as she wandered deeper into the labyrinth of alleys. Torn paper fluttered along the ground, its movement like dying birds struggling for life. The air carried a taste of reckoning, a sharpness that clung to everything like rust on metal.

She moved through the darkened streets like a bat, eyes closed but somehow making her way. I kept my distance, the hunger sharpening with every step. She didn't even notice me, didn't care that I was there.

This was now my ritual. A sacrament of pursuit. I stalked her like prey, my footsteps measured and silent. Scripture danced through my mind; passages conformed into weapons.

I kept my distance, following the stagger of her silhouette as she moved deeper into the city's shadows. She didn't look back—none of them ever did. They walked like the world had already turned its back on them.

Psalm 1:6 lingered in my mind, carried by the echoes of my grandfather's sermons: "For the Lord knows the way of the righteous, but the way of the wicked shall perish." Back then, the words were just scripture—phrases spoken from the pulpit, heavy with tradition but stripped of meaning. I was too young to understand, too sheltered to grasp what it truly meant for the wicked to fall. But now, I understood. It wasn't just scripture—it was permission. A directive passed down from hands far greater than mine. The wicked would perish; it was written, not as suggestion, but as fate. And maybe, just maybe, I was meant to be the instrument of that fate.

I convinced myself it wasn't violence—it was obedience. A scripture etched in fragile pages, waiting for someone to read between the lines. To understand that faith sometimes demanded more than prayer. It demanded action. It demanded sacrifice. And I was willing to give it.

So, when she stumbled into the alley by the train yard, her legs buckling beneath the weight of her sins, it felt like divine alignment. I watched her crash against the wall, sliding down to the damp concrete, knees pulled to her chest like a child retreating from the world. The shadows here were thick, pressing in from all sides like sentinels, muffling the noise of the city, swallowing her cries before they could even form. It was perfect—hidden from judgment, cloaked in silence.

The knife pulsed in my grip, its weight an anchor, tethering me to the moment—sharp, unyielding, inevitable. It wasn't just a blade—it was a promise. A confession written in steel. I stepped forward, my movements deliberate, measured, each footfall a recitation of that verse. The way of the wicked shall perish. The words hummed beneath my skin, guiding me closer, steadying my breath. The blade pulsed in my grip, its need entwined with mine—a single purpose, sharpened and absolute.

She saw me then. Her head snapped up, breath catching in her throat. She shrank back, pressing herself against the brick like she could disappear into it. Fear tightened her features, making her look younger, vulnerable. I almost paused. Almost. But the verse rang in my ears, louder than her trembling voice. The way of the wicked shall perish. Her hands went up, palms facing me, shaking. "Please," she whispered, the words frayed and watery. "I—I just need a place to sleep. Just... just leave me alone."

Her plea hung in the air, thin and weightless. I stood over her, the knife steady in my hand. Everything else melted away—her voice, the distant rattle of the train yard, the hum of streetlights. It was just me, her, and the promise of redemption. I took a step forward, the scripture unfurling in my thoughts, binding my movements to something ancient. For the Lord knows the way of the righteous... My grip tightened. Her breath hitched. I watched her eyes flicker with desperation, her body curling in on itself like she was trying to become smaller, trying to disappear. But there was nowhere to go. There was never anywhere to go.

The blade floated between us, its edge gleaming in the fractured light. But the way of the wicked shall perish. The words threaded through my thoughts, stitching purpose to flesh. I didn't even feel my hand move. The blade met skin, slid through without resistance. Her gasp caught in her throat, eyes widening with the shock of it. I watched her body go slack, her hands clawing at the brick for purchase. Her breath came in short, ragged bursts, each one fainter than the last. I felt the blade pulse in my hand, the shiver of satisfaction that came with it. The scripture hummed beneath my skin, warm and steady. I stepped back, watched the light fade from her body as if it had never been there at all.

I left her crumpled in the alley, her body folded into itself like the city had swallowed her whole. My footsteps echoed off the brick, the knife still warm in my hand. Psalm 1:6 played through my mind with each step, a benediction for the righteous.

For a moment, I almost believed it.

The way of the wicked shall perish. I whispered it to myself as I walked away, letting the words coil around my thoughts, squeezing out the doubt. I wanted it to be true. I wanted to believe that what I had done was more than just violence—it was purification. I held onto that feeling all the way home, cradling it like something fragile. But truth has a way of slipping through your fingers. By morning, the hunger had returned, sharper than before. And then I saw her name.

The newspapers called her Helen. I remember seeing it in print, black letters against yellowing newsprint, like it had been carved into stone. They said she was in her fifties. An old woman whose life had unraveled under the weight of desperation. I studied the article, its words clinical and cold, just enough detail to move on to the next tragedy. They found her body slumped near the train yard, waiting against the bricks like she'd been placed there. The write-up was buried in the back pages, squeezed between obituaries and ads for used furniture. A footnote. That's all she became. A name. A number. A silhouette they washed from the concrete and forgot.

I told myself it was justice—that she was another thread in the sickness spreading through the city, something that needed to be cut loose. But the truth was sharper, more honest: I needed her to disappear. If she became just another forgotten name, another body chalked up to the rot festering in the city's veins, then what I did was simply the inevitable—a transaction between life and silence. It made sense. It felt righteous. I convinced myself I was purging something unclean, burning away the filth like a sacrificial fire. But even as I fed myself that lie, the doubt crept in, slow and deliberate, like smoke seeping through the cracks. Maybe it wasn't cleansing. Maybe it was something else. Something I couldn't name.

The feeling didn't fade. It never did. It burned beneath my skin, simmering just out of reach, pulling at me with a whisper I couldn't shake. At first, I called it purpose—divine permission handed down from scripture. I recited verses to myself, clung to them like lifelines, let the words burrow into the hollow spaces. But it wasn't purpose I felt—it was need. A hunger that grew sharper each time it was fed. I watched addicts chasing something that always slipped away. I used to pity them, used to believe I was different. But maybe I wasn't.

Maybe it wasn't justice I craved. Maybe it was the feeling. The release. The rush of control, pure and unfiltered, flooding my veins the way heroin did hers. I saw it in my hands sometimes—the way they shook when too much time had passed. The way my thoughts circled back to it, unbidden and relentless. Maybe it wasn't righteousness that moved me—maybe it was compulsion. The very thing I condemned in others, I harbored in myself. But I didn't want to stop. Maybe I couldn't.

I told myself it was different—that I was different. But the truth lingered just beneath the surface, festering and raw. My mother poisoned herself with needles and smoke. WasI poisoning myself with violence? And just like her, I kept going back. Not because I wanted to. Because I needed to. And maybe that made me just like them. Maybe it made me worse.

The next day, I dug a grave behind my grandparents' shed. The shovel bit into the earth with each thrust, dirt piling up in brittle clumps, cracking open like old wounds. The blade lay beside me, its edge nicked and stained, still sticky with what it had taken. I wrapped it in the shirt I'd worn that night—ripped, blood-specked, and heavy with the memory of it. It looked smaller in my hands, almost harmless. I covered it slowly, handful by handful, the earth swallowing it inch by inch. The dirt settled with a sigh, like it was taking back something that never should have been found.

But the burial felt like blasphemy. I stared at the mound of dirt, waiting for something—punishment, absolution, a sign that what I had done was righteous. But there was only the wind, curling through the weeds, brushing over the fresh earth like it hadn't even noticed. It felt like I was trying to suffocate the purity I had just embraced. Like covering the blade was an attempt to silence what it had given me. The hunger only swelled, its absence sharpening my need until it threatened to consume me. I craved another offering. A ritual to reaffirm my purpose.

I held a funeral. Not with prayers or hymns, but with silence. I stood over the grave, the dirt still fresh and loose, and imagined the knife's craving buried with it, stifled beneath the weight of the earth. I tried to believe it was over. That the hunger would be satisfied, at least for a while. But even then, I knew it was a lie. The knife was gone, but what it fed had only been starved. The ritual did nothing but sharpen my desires, stretching them taut and thin until they buzzed just beneath my skin.

What I mistook for peace was nothing more than a moment of quiet—a counterfeit salvation that left the need more ravenous each time it returned. Satisfaction decayed into a bottomless pit, then back to that endless ache. It felt like feeding an addiction I could never satisfy. And for the first time, I wondered if this was all I'd ever be. If the ache would be the only constant in my life.

I prayed that night. Not for forgiveness, but for clarity. For a sign that what I was doing was righteous. I wanted to believe it so desperately. Needed to believe it. But there was nothing. Just silence. A void that swallowed my prayers and left me stranded in its emptiness.

And from that emptiness, something grew. A

restless ache, stirred by the quiet, blossoming into something unknown. The burial had changed nothing. The need was still there, brewing within me, starving and impatient.

The hunger clawed at me with increasing ferocity. I searched the newspapers for any mention of my offering, but the city moved on, indifferent and blind. If no one saw my sacrifice, was it even real? The thought festered, pushing me to seek another. To leave a mark so deep that no one could overlook it.

The unrest followed me into the new year, relentless and simmering beneath the surface. It was the ache that led me to her, a young homeless woman I found wandering under the EL. She was like so many others I had watched drift through the city, unseen and unwanted. But something about her pulled me in.

With her, I wanted to try something different. I thought that maybe if I unraveled her story—really saw her for who she was—it might change what came after. Maybe understanding her would dull the need, shift the craving into something less consuming. I wasn't sure if it would work, but I was willing to try. So, I offered her a kindness I didn't truly feel—a cheap bottle of wine I'd swiped from my grandfather's collection and a few words that sounded like care. She followed me without hesitation, stumbling alongside me through the narrow alleys near Pratt Street. I wondered if maybe, just maybe, there was another way to fix what was broken.

"Where do you sleep?" I asked, echoing the questions I'd been asked by teachers and counselors who thought kindness could heal anything.

"Wherever the city lets me," she replied, her voice ragged but steady. "Under the bridges, alleyways, wherever it's quiet enough." Her answer was bare—no excuses, no pretense, just the raw truth of it.

"What do you dream about?" I pressed, softer this time, almost curious. I thought that maybe if I could pull back the layers, if I could see the person beneath, it might shift something inside me. Make the need fade.

"Dreams?" She laughed, a sound that was more disbelief than humor. "Dreams are for people who have something worth waking up to."

Her words hit harder than I expected. I tried to picture her with something to wake up to—a place, a person, anything that could tether her to the world instead of drifting through its cracks. For a moment, I almost wanted it for her. Maybe knowing her would change everything. Maybe I didn't have to be the end of her story.

"Do you ever feel like the city's trying to swallow you whole?" I asked, my voice quieter, almost hesitant.

She nodded, not looking at me, her fingers curling tighter around the bottle. "Every damn day," she whispered.

For the first time, I wondered if there was another way. If I could change what came after—not just for her, but for me. If seeing her as more than just another offering would be enough to quiet the thing gnawing at me. Maybe understanding her could be a way out. Maybe redemption wasn't just found in blood.

And I understood. Not just her words, but the weight behind them. It was the same ache I carried—an emptiness clawing from the inside. In that moment, I wasn't just watching her. I was recognizing myself. And somewhere in that recognition, a decision was already forming.

"Do you feel like taking a walk?" I asked, my tone gentle, coaxing. "Sometimes it helps. Just...moving. Getting away from everything."

Her eyes uncertain, but she nodded. "Yeah...maybe. Maybe that'd be nice."

There was no place to go. Just the open air and the quiet of the night. We ended up near an abandoned fruit stand, where crates and debris littered the ground like forgotten relics. She laughed with a jittery edge, her words tumbling out in fragments, brittle and scattered. As if she couldn't believe someone was willing to listen to her ramblings. She didn't realize I wasn't listening. I was studying her pauses, her pain, the places where her voice cracked.

"What happened to you?"

Her eyes flickered, unsure if I meant it or if I was mocking her. But desperation won out.

"Same as everyone else. Life chewed me up and spit me out." She forced a laugh, the sound brittle and empty.

I pressed, like the counselors had pressed me. Like the teachers who called me troubled.

"No family? No friends?"

"Family's dead. Or gone. Not much difference, is there?" Another hollow laugh. She didn't even care that I was a stranger. It was enough that someone was asking."

I kept nodding, offering her interest like faded warmth to a chilled soul. Making her feel seen. Her voice grew softer, words bleeding together as the wine took hold.

She was younger than the others. Her skin filthy from living outside, hair tangled and matted. Her eyes held a vacancy, a desolate stillness that reflected the ache within me. It stirred something restless, relentless as the tide.

"I used to have dreams. They just never fit right." She said as she turned her back to me, her voice slurring into something incoherent, words spilling out and crashing into each other like they didn't know where to go. Her movements unsteady, arms flailing to catch some invisible balance. She mumbled things I couldn't understand—fragments of conversations that never happened, apologies to people who weren't there. There was a softness in her voice, something cracked and childlike. I almost spoke. Almost asked her if she needed help. But the words died in my throat.

That's when I saw it—a jagged piece of metal, half-buried in the grime and refuse, its edge rusted but still sharp enough to tear. A broken fragment discarded by the city, just like her. I stood there, frozen for a breath too long, staring at that twisted shard. It felt like it was looking back, like it had been waiting. My heart thudded against my ribs, my fingers twitching with the need to pick it up. But I didn't. Not yet. I just watched her sway, her back to me, shoulders hunched under the weight of some invisible burden. She stumbled, caught herself, then kept walking, her feet dragging through the dirt like she was wading through water. The shard glinted under the flickering streetlight, and something in my mind clicked.

This was meant to be.

I could hear my grandfather's voice from those

Sunday sermons, his hands raised high, eyes wild with conviction: 'The Lord shall go before thee, and the God of Israel shall be thy rear guard.' I swallowed hard, the verse sticking in my throat. He always said that signs were laid out before the faithful, if only they had the eyes to see them. I looked down at the shard, rusted and jagged, its edges glimmering with the pale light of the moon. It had been waiting there, discarded and overlooked—until I came. Until I found it. Or maybe...it found me.

Her shoulders sagged, spine curling inward like something beaten down by years of disappointment. She paused, leaned against the wall as if the air itself had grown heavy, pressing her into the bricks. Her breathing was labored, each inhale like she was sucking in shards of glass. I watched her for a long moment, feeling the weight of my own breath, the stillness of the night settling over us. I could have walked away. Left her there to sink back into the city, to drift and decay. But the hunger didn't care about mercy. The craving tightened in my chest, curling around my heart like wire. It wouldn't let me leave.

I stepped forward, my movements deliberate, slow. My breath came shallow, pulse hammering beneath my skin. I knelt down, fingers closing around the shard. It bit into my palm as I pried it free, the jagged edge slicing into my flesh. I didn't flinch. I welcomed it. The pain felt righteous, like penance. I held the metal up to the light, watching the way it gleamed with a dull, brutal sheen. The city was silent around me, waiting. Even the wind seemed to still. I felt my breath catch, my mind stumbling over the weight of what I was about to do. But I couldn't stop.

I moved toward her, the shard steady in my grip. She hadn't noticed me yet. Her back was still turned, shoulders hunched as she murmured to herself, the words muddled and thick. I was three steps away when she turned. Her eyes met mine, and for a split second, I saw something there— recognition. Not of me, but of the end. Her mouth opened, a whisper of breath escaping. "Wait," she said, her voice trembling. "I—I'm just tired. I just need somewhere to sleep. Please..."

My fingers tightened around the shard. My mind screamed at me to walk away. To leave her there. But then she stepped forward, her hand outstretched. "I used to have a son," she whispered, her voice breaking. "He'd be your age by now. If—if I hadn't lost him." She extended her hand to pinch my cheek. "You remind me of him," she added, her eyes glassy, swimming with something too heavy to name. "You—you got his eyes."

She trailed off, the words slipping away. "I used to tell him to keep his head up. To stay out of places like this." She let out a breath, sharp and jagged. "Guess that makes me a liar."

My fingers dug into the shard, metal slicing deeper, blood pooling along my knuckles. I should have walked away. I knew it then. I could have left her to whatever ghosts she was whispering to. But the craving wouldn't let me. It roared in my chest, pushing me forward. Urging me on. I stepped closer, and her eyes flicked back open, locking onto mine. "I'm sorry," I whispered, the words coming out before I could stop them. "You were chosen."

Her mouth opened, breath slipping out in a shudder. "Chosen for what?" she asked, her voice barely a whisper. I didn't answer. Couldn't. The craving tightened around me, and the shard found her flesh before I even knew I had moved. The sound it made was soft—like a sigh escaping her body. Her hands clawed at the air, fingers scraping brick, leaving smears of red that caught the moonlight. I pulled the shard free, and something inside me trembled. A shiver that ran from the tips of my fingers to the back of my neck. It felt...different. Sharp and electric. A wave of warmth flooded through me, building and crashing, rolling over me in pulses. I gasped, stumbling back, the shard still slick in my hand.

I struck again. And again. The rhythm came naturally, like a prayer I'd been reciting my whole life. Each thrust sent another tremor through me, deeper, more consuming. It wasn't just satisfaction. It was something else. My breath came out in ragged bursts, my vision blurring at the edges. The world narrowed to the point of the blade, the give of her flesh, the wet sound of metal meeting bone. And with each motion, the sensation grew stronger, cresting like a wave ready to break. When the final thrust landed, the tremor hit me full force. My body shuddered, breath catching, every nerve ending sparking with something that felt like fire and relief all at once. I stumbled back, gasping, my hands shaking. The shard slipped from my grip, clattering to the ground.

I stood there for a long time, staring down at her body crumpled on the concrete, limbs twisted, mouth half-open like she was still trying to finish her sentence. The warmth still pulsed through me, fading slowly, like embers cooling after the blaze. I took a breath and it felt clean. Sharp. The craving was gone. For now. But something else had taken its place.

I didn't know what it was then. I couldn't name it. But I knew I would feel it again. And I knew I would want to.

As I discarded the shard, the tremor still lingered in my fingertips, pulsing through my veins like the aftershock of something holy. My breath came out in ragged bursts, every inhale sharper than the last, like the air itself had been cut open. I stared at my hands—sticky and trembling, painted with what she'd left behind. The warmth still simmered beneath my skin, radiating out from my core, spreading through my limbs in waves. My knees felt weak, like they might buckle beneath the weight of it. But it wasn't fear. It wasn't shock. It was something I'd never felt before. Something deeper.

My hands shook as I braced myself against the brick wall, the rough surface biting into my palms, grounding me to the moment. My breath hitched, catching in my throat as that pulse rolled through me again, stronger this time, spreading from the base of my spine to my fingertips. It felt like fire. Like my blood had turned electric, humming through my body, lighting up every nerve, every thought. My vision blurred at the edges, tunneling down to the slick surface of the concrete where her blood pooled, still warm, still moving. It gleamed in the moonlight, dark and viscous, spreading out in thin rivers, carving paths through the grime. I watched it flow, mesmerized, feeling the rhythm of my heart sync with its slow crawl across the pavement.

And that's when I understood. That tremor. That shiver that crawled up my spine and bloomed behind my eyes. It wasn't just satisfaction. It was more. So much more. It was devotion. A sacrament carved out of flesh and bone, written in blood. My first orgasm—ripped from me not by lust or longing, but by purpose. It shook me to my core, a revelation that left me gasping, clutching at the wall as the waves crashed over me, one after the other, relentless and pure. I'd read about it before, heard whispers of what it was supposed to feel like, but this—this was different. This wasn't a release. It was a ceremony.

The realization stole my breath, left me dizzy and swaying. My knees buckled, and I sank against the brick, hands still shaking, body still humming with that strange, electric warmth. I wasn't just taking something from her—I was being filled. Every drop of her blood, every tremor of her death had poured back into me, filling the hollow spaces I hadn't even known were there. It wasn't flesh that satisfied me. It wasn't lust. It was purpose. It was the knowing—the absolute certainty that I was meant to do this. That the blade wasn't just an object, but an instrument. A key to something bigger.

My breath evened out, slow and steady, the tremor finally fading from my hands. I let go of the wall, standing upright, staring down at her lifeless form. The city stretched out around us, indifferent and unfeeling, and for the first time, I felt like I belonged to it. Like I understood its language. Its needs. Its hunger. I hadn't just killed her. I had become something new. Something sacred.

This was worship. Pure and undiluted. A revelation carved through violence, sanctified in blood. And in that moment, I knew—I would never stop. I would never want to. Because now I understood. The craving wasn't a sickness. It was salvation. And I would follow it wherever it led me.

This was only the beginning, a passage from innocence to understanding. Blood was scripture, and I had only begun to write.

I had lost my virginity—not in the way talked about in school hallways, but something deeper. Purer. Like I had surrendered myself to something sacred. A rite of passage carved in flesh. I felt it settle into my bones, crawl beneath my skin, thread itself through my veins like it had always been there, waiting.

A bloodlust rose within me—not as rage, but as

rapture. An unholy consummation. A gospel inked in violence. I had felt its rhythm, its pulse, like it was drawing me closer with each breath, each heartbeat. The air tasted sharper, every sound crisper, as if the world itself had shifted to accommodate this new truth. Colors bled richer. The concrete beneath my feet felt more solid, more real. The city had opened its arms to me, finally recognizing me as its own.

For the first time, I felt whole. Like I had finally shed the brittle shell of innocence and stepped into something real. Something raw and undeniable. The craving was not just part of me; it was me. It had always been there, waiting for me to discover it, waiting for me to accept it. I had been afraid before. Of its hunger. Of its whispers. But fear had been replaced by understanding. By devotion.

I relived it over and over, letting the memory unfold in fragments—her gasp, the tearing of flesh, the rush of sensation that coursed through me like flames. It was sacred. It was scripture.

A truth I could not unsee.

For a moment, the craving lay dormant but restless. A quiet that trembled with anticipation.

That feast had left me full and satisfied, but it wasn't enough. I needed to see it acknowledged. I craved the proof that what I'd done wasn't just real, but something worthy of notice.

I needed to see the headlines.

I devoured the ink like sustenance, desperate to see my offering in print—as if each word could nourish the hunger still stirring beneath my skin. I needed validation. Proof that what I'd done mattered, that my actions had been seen and acknowledged.

The newspapers called it the most gruesome murder of the year.

They marveled at the brutality, the sheer number of wounds inflicted—seventy-four, they reported. The savagery that left her body unrecognizable, her remains found beneath a storage truck near a fruit stand on Pratt Street, discovered by a restaurant employee on their morning shift. A headline. A horror that stirred something within me.

But even in the glow of satisfaction, something nagged at me. A story I couldn't ignore. Harrison Graham. A man whose crimes eclipsed mine, his hunger painted across the pages with the same reverence they used to describe my offering. A murderer who preyed upon women and buried their bodies within his own home. A man who killed without remorse.

He was a man whose hunger mirrored my own, painted by the newspapers as a madman—an abomination. But their condemnation only fueled my curiosity. Was his hunger the same as mine? Or was he nothing but a beast without purpose? I needed to know if his bloodlust carried the same righteousness, the same devotion. Or if I alone held the purity of purpose.

I scoured the papers, searching for every mention of him. I needed to understand. To see if the hunger he fed was the same as mine.

I devoured every word about him. Pored over each article until his name felt like an echo of my own. They called him mad, broken, a creature driven by sickness. But I saw something more— someone who had embraced the hunger instead of hiding from it.

And I wondered if I could do the same.

But if he was captured, then he was flawed. Weak. Perhaps his hunger had consumed him because he failed to give it purpose. Or maybe the city simply couldn't see the beauty in his devotion. Either way, his failure was a warning. A lesson. If I were to embrace the hunger, I needed to be more. Smarter. Sharper. My hunger would be holy. Controlled. Eternal.

I spent nights unraveling the fragments of his story. Graham's victims were found in various stages of decomposition, their bodies discarded like forgotten relics. But there was a method to his madness. A pattern. He chose the broken, the discarded, the desperate.

Much like me.

I couldn't help but draw comparisons. His bloodlust had consumed him to the point of madness. He surrounded himself with death, clinging to his victims even after their final breath. And yet, I saw something almost beautiful in his compulsion. A dedication. A surrender to the hunger.

It made me question my own restraint. The boundaries I had tried to impose on myself since moving in with my grandparents. Church.

Prayer. Their futile attempts to cleanse me of what I was becoming.

But what if I didn't want to be cleansed?

I told myself I was better than Graham. That I had purpose, direction. I wasn't killing out of madness or loneliness. I was cleansing the city, cutting away the filth before it could spread.

But the truth twisted itself around me like a snake.

What if my hunger was no different than his? What if the satisfaction I craved was nothing more than an illusion, a lie I told myself to justify the blood I spilled?

Harrison Graham was caught. They dragged him out of his apartment, his eyes wild, his clothes stained with the remnants of his compulsion. They called him a beast. A demon. They locked him away and boasted of their triumph.

But even as they paraded their victory, I couldn't help but feel a kinship with the man they called a monster.

Because I knew the hunger wasn't something that could be locked away. It wasn't something that could be cured or purged by the rituals of religion.

It was part of me. And the more I tried to bury it, the stronger it grew into obsession.

And in that obsession, I realized something. I didn't want to be cured. I wanted to embrace the hunger. To feed it. To become the thing I was always meant to be.

The craving didn't just live inside me—it grew, stretching itself through my veins, settling in my bones. It whispered promises of purpose, of becoming something more than just a boy pretending to be normal. The first time, it had been rage. The second, it was revelation. But now, it was a calling. The need wasn't just physical—it was spiritual. A gospel written in flesh.

My grandfather's sermons would come back to me in fragments, verses stitched together from years of Sunday mornings spent beneath the gaze of a bleeding Christ. "He will purify the sons of Levi and refine them like gold and silver, and they will bring offerings in righteousness to the Lord." The hunger thrummed beneath my ribs, the craving clawing its way to the surface. I wasn't just purging the streets. I was making offerings. I was the righteous blade.

I began to understand that the hunger was not a curse. It was a gift. A sign. I didn't need to fight it; I needed to listen. To follow it. Each pulse of need, each thought of temptation was a call to arms. It was my duty to answer. It wasn't about rage anymore—it was about purpose. A purpose I couldn't deny. A purpose I couldn't escape.

There was no going back. No repentance. No salvation. Only the Bloodlust. And the promise of feeding it. I looked out over the city that night, its lights shimmering like stars cast into filth. And I felt nothing but anticipation. The craving simmered beneath my skin, whispering promises of what was to come. It wasn't rage. It wasn't revenge. It was clarity. It was purpose.

Romans 6:23 — "For the wages of sin is death; but the gift of God is eternal life through Jesus Christ our Lord."

I whispered the verse under my breath, feeling it spill from my lips like confession. It didn't feel like damnation. It felt like truth.

Death was the price of sin. And I was the collector. The harvester. The righteous blade cutting away the decay.

This was my truth.
This was my gospel.
My ministry.
My calling.

THOU SHALT TAKE WHAT TEMPTS

January 1989

Poem - The Purge of Saints

They say the righteous walk in
light, Their steps ordered by
heaven's grace.

But what of those who tread in
night, Whose faith is blood, whose
truth's embrace?

I am the blade, I am the hand, The
gospel writ in scarlet stains.

Salvation torn from bone and
strand; A savior crowned in
sinners' veins.

The altar built of flesh and sin, A
temple made of screams and dust.

Forgiveness lost, where hell
begins, My gospel forged by pain
and lust.

I drink the darkness, swallow
rage, A beast reborn with every
sin.

Their blood the ink, my soul the
page, A covenant never meant to
end.

Faith twisted into something vile,
A savior cloaked in sinner's guise.

I wear their terror with a smile,
Their deaths my truth, their pain
my prize.

I stood at the threshold of Terry's apartment, my
hand resting on the chipped wooden frame. I
don't remember how long I lingered there,

listening to the muffled hum of her television vibrating through the thin walls, feeling the vibrations thrum beneath my fingertips. Something stirred beneath my skin—slow, deliberate, curling through my veins like smoke. It wasn't just anticipation. It was something heavier, something that held tight and refused to let go. With her, it was different. I didn't want to admit it—not then, not even to myself—but there was something about the way she moved, the way she laughed, that stayed with me long after she left Goldie's.

She wasn't like the others. She moved through that place like she didn't belong to it, slipping through the door as if she were searching for something just out of reach. A drink, maybe. An escape. Or maybe she was running from the inevitable like the rest of them. But she swam on the edge of their world, never fully crossing over. I think that's what drew me in—her refusal to drown.

I wanted to know why. I wanted to unravel that secret, to understand what kept her head above water when the rest of them sank without a fight. She carried herself differently—shoulders back, chin high—like the rot that clung to the sidewalks hadn't touched her. It fascinated me. It infuriated me. I watched her for days, mapping the rhythm of her life. The way she swayed when she walked, the laughter that spilled from her lips like it belonged to another world, the way her fingers moved when she spoke. I memorized the curve of her smile, the lightness in her step. I told myself it was study—preparation. But it wasn't. It was preservation.

She was alive in a way that made me feel raw and unguarded. Human. I hated that feeling. I had buried it long ago—sealed it off with ritual and resolve, layered it beneath justification and purpose. But with her, it crept back in, slow and insidious, threading itself through my thoughts until it burned. She reminded me of everything I could never touch—everything that lingered just outside of my grasp.

Maybe that's why I was there, standing at her door, my pulse thrumming with something that felt like hope twisted in on itself. Maybe it wasn't just the hunger. Maybe it was something deeper. A need to claim what I couldn't have. To hold it, if only for a moment, before it slipped away. I told myself it was cleansing. That I was purifying something broken. But I think now that was just another lie I learned to live with. I didn't want to purify her. I wanted to possess her. I wanted to keep her suspended in that place where the rot hadn't touched her yet, where her laughter still felt like it belonged to something pure. I wanted to own that moment before the world had its chance to ruin it.

The door was unlocked. Careless. Or maybe just hopeful. I remember standing there, my hand on the knob, feeling the weight of choice settle against my palm. I could have walked away. I could have buried that hunger beneath routine and ritual, smothered it before it could spread. But I didn't. I stepped inside, shutting the door softly behind me, sealing us both in. The air was thick with the scent of old perfume and cigarette smoke, the kind of smell that clings to you, seeps into your pores, and lingers long after you've left. Her apartment was cluttered—trinkets and ashtrays scattered across every surface, remnants of moments she'd tried to hold on to. I imagined her here, sifting through fragments of her life, trying to make sense of it all.

For a moment, I just watched her. She was sitting on the edge of her bed, her head bowed over a pile of photographs. The soft glow of a lamp spilled across her skin, painting her in delicate shadows. I felt something twist inside me— regret, maybe, or longing. It clawed at the edges of my resolve, whispering that I didn't have to do this. That maybe she could be spared. I didn't understand it then, and I'm not sure I do now. All I know is that it made me hesitate. For a single breath, I almost turned back. But the hunger was louder. It always was.

She looked up, eyes blinking with confusion. There was no fear at first. Just the slow, dawning realization that I wasn't supposed to be there.

"Who...who the hell are you?" she asked, her voice slurred from sleep or alcohol. Maybe both.

The question struck me deeper than I expected. Who am I? Her words landed between us like a splinter, sharp and unwanted. How could she not know? I had followed her for weeks, memorized the rhythm of her life, mapped the curve of her smile, the sway of her walk. I knew the way she folded her hands when she spoke, the way she brushed the hair from her face when she laughed. I knew her. More than anyone else ever had. More than she even knew herself.

But she didn't know me. Not even a flicker of recognition. I stood there, rooted to the spot, feeling that realization twist inside me, like a blade turning slow and purposeful. All those moments I had captured—frozen in my mind like still frames—and to her, I was nothing but a stranger.

So I didn't answer. Words felt like wasted breath. I moved forward, my weight bearing her down onto the bed. Her hands flailed, fists striking against my shoulders, but there was no real strength behind them. Not enough to matter. I remember feeling the tension leave her body as if she understood—like she knew there was no point in fighting back.

I had learned from before—there would be no trace, no mistakes. The knife drove into her chest, carving through skin and sinew with a wet, primitive sound. Her body arched beneath me, spasming in a grotesque mimicry of life. Heat spilled over my hands, thick and unyielding, seeping between my fingers. But it wasn't the violence that left me breathless—it was the intimacy.

There was a fragility in those last moments, the way her pulse fluttered against my grip, stubborn and unrelenting. It clung to life in a way that felt defiant, almost holy. I remember wondering what it must feel like—to want to hold on that badly.

To fight against the end when everything around you is telling you to let go.

It felt like possession. Like I had taken something that didn't belong to me, something pure and untouched by the rot of Goldie's. Her life pooled between my fingers, warm and alive, and for a moment, I felt something I couldn't name — something dangerously close to love.

But that wasn't possible. Love didn't fit in my world. Love wasn't something you took; it was something you were given. And I had never been given anything. But possession — that was different. That was something you could force into existence, something you could hold onto, even if it meant breaking it in your grip. I think I knew then that I wasn't purifying her. I was preserving her. Keeping her from the corruption that would surely come. At least with me, she could remain untouched. Perfect. Mine.

When it was over, I sat beside her, my hands still slick with her warmth. I stared at her for a long time, trying to understand what I had taken, what I had left behind. I told myself it was justice. I told myself it was purpose. But the truth clung to my skin, sharp and unyielding. I wanted her to belong to me. I wanted to possess her, to own something pure before the world stripped it away. But it was gone now, and I was alone again.

I think about that sometimes—the way I tried to twist it into something righteous, something holy. But it wasn't. Not with her. It was greed. It was hunger. And I surrendered to it willingly.

Diary Entry: January 20, 1989

It's been years since my last offering, a silence that stretched too long, almost unbearable. But last night broke the quiet, rekindled something vital inside me. The act was special, intimate, unlike anything I'd done before. Terry was more than a mere offering; she was a revelation, a testament to my true calling. Her death was my masterpiece, a carefully chosen moment that reignited the virtue of my purpose.

Yet today, the city speaks of the Frankford Slasher again. They attribute my sacred work to him, a monster whose brutality lacks grace, whose actions are uncontrolled and messy. Some of his claimed kills were mine, others not. His actions disgust me—lacking precision, reason, and divine purpose. It infuriates me to see my truth muddled, distorted by association with his senseless violence.

But this confusion ends now. After Terry, there can be no doubt, no mistake. My offering is righteous, my violence pure. His deceit mocks my purpose.

They're still talking about the Frankford Slasher. The newspapers scream his name, painting him as a monster lurking in shadows, snatching away lives as if he owned them. Some of those murders were mine. Others weren't. But his kills—messy, brutal, devoid of divine reason—could never be mistaken for mine. It makes me angry to see my acts confused with his. Each action of

my mercy is a carefully chosen
sacrifice in service of something
greater.

But today will be different.
Yesterday's act will set things
right, unmistakably mine. No
longer will they confuse my work
with his brutality.

"Cursed be he that doeth the work
of the Lord deceitfully." - Jeremiah
48:10

His deceit mocks my purpose.
Soon enough, they'll see clearly.

They will know the truth. They
will know me.

Reflecting on that entry now, it all seems so
distant. But the anger still burns—raw,
consuming, unyielding. In April 1990, they
arrested a man named Leonard Christopher for
the murders—including mine. His violence was
filthy, driven by nothing but sick impulses. Mine
were different—sacrifices made to cleanse the city
of its filth. Their ignorance, their failure to see the
difference, sickened me. They had tarnished my

truth, obscured my purpose. I felt robbed. And I would teach them the difference. One sacrifice at a time.

They couldn't see it. They couldn't grasp my artistry. Leonard's brutality was a blunt instrument, a wild swing in the dark, flailing with feral impulses that splattered without thought. His violence was chaos—unmeasured, unworthy. A tantrum dressed as terror. They called him a monster with reverence, his name spoken as if he had crafted something worthy of fear.

But my work was different. Precision. Talent. Every stroke deliberate, every breath measured. A consecration carved in flesh—a cleansing they would never understand. And yet, they polluted my purpose, twisting it into his savagery. Their blindness only deepened my resolve. They would see me. They would understand.

How could they not recognize the precision? The care? The purpose?
They were blind to the beauty I brought to their rotting world. And I would make them see.

Leonard's arrest should have felt like victory—a purge of the filth they had smeared across my name. And in a way, it did. For the first time in months, I could breathe easier. Terry and Helen had faces now, and it wasn't mine. The city had its monster, neatly wrapped up and paraded in front of flashing cameras. The relief settled over me like a shroud, numbing the tension that had coiled tight beneath my skin.

But relief wasn't enough. It never was. Their blindness was almost laughable—how easily they accepted his capture, how quickly they stitched his name to my work. I let that ignorance soothe me, let it bury the whispers of doubt and wrap me in stillness. For a while, it was enough just to be invisible.

But invisibility breeds hunger. His capture had gifted me the perfect opportunity—the city would be on edge, but they'd be looking in the wrong direction. Their eyes would follow his trail, and I would move through the shadows untouched.

Weeks passed. I read the papers religiously, absorbing every detail of his arrest. His face plastered across the front pages, headlines screaming his name like it was some kind of triumph. They dissected his crimes with smug certainty, spinning their tales from podiums and news desks—safe, sterile places far from the streets he prowled. Their sensationalized language was a spectacle, a carefully constructed narrative. They spoke of his depravity as if it mirrored mine. As if we were bound by the same hunger.

But he wasn't me. He couldn't be. His violence was filthy, driven by desperation and impulse, each victim defiled and discarded with thoughtless abandon. Where was the grace in that? Where was the devotion? His work was chaos—unmeasured, obscene. A tantrum splattered in blood, nothing more. A mockery of everything I had created.

But they needed him. They needed someone like him to fill that role. They had the sketch—a white man. A composite drawn from witnesses, plastered across bulletin boards and late-night news segments. They had whispers of a different kind of monster stalking the city. But when it came time to pin it on someone, they chose him. The sketch didn't matter. His skin did.

Because that's how it always is. The city breathes easier when its monsters are wrapped in Black skin. It makes it easier for them to believe. It doesn't matter that two of those bodies were mine and the rest belonged to someone else. It doesn't matter that the composite sketch stared back with pale skin and sharp features. The newspapers forgot. The witnesses forgot. The city forgot.

He was just their scapegoat. And he was mine. They needed him to be guilty. His capture bought me time, gave me room to breathe. I read their headlines and felt something close to relief. They had their monster, and it wasn't me.

Their narrative was complete, their fear contained, and that meant I was free. Free to continue the work. Free to cleanse without their eyes on me. Their blindness became my liberation, their desperation my cover.

They painted him with my sins, dressed him in my shadow, and washed my hands clean.

The newspapers screamed his name, splashed his face across their front pages like a victory cry. For weeks, they had debated, speculated—was he the true monster, or just another shadow in the dark? But when the handcuffs clicked shut, the city exhaled, sinking back into its own rot, content with the illusion of safety. They had their person. The hunt was over. The shadows grew still, their whispers silenced.

About four months had slipped by since his arrest. The city returned to its rhythm, its streets crowded with familiar faces—hollow-eyed addicts, stumbling drunks, bodies dragging themselves from one corner to the next. But none of them felt right. None of them sparked that familiar need.

I watched. I waited. The city pulsed with its own kind of life, stretching out its arms to pull in the broken and the desperate. My patience wore thin, my steps tracing the same pathways, circling the same places. I was careful, deliberate, waiting for something that mattered. But still...nothing. The right one hadn't appeared.

Until she did.

I saw her beneath the streetlight, her figure catching the glow in a way that seemed almost unreal. Dark hair spilled over her shoulders, catching the light and shimmering like it didn't belong to the grime-streaked sidewalks she walked on. Her eyes drifted, far away from the mess around her, like she had walked into a world she didn't recognize. She didn't belong here—an unfamiliar sight in a place that had long since forgotten beauty.

I followed, my footsteps measured and steady. I watched the way she moved, the way her gaze skimmed over the broken asphalt as if she were untouched by the ugliness around her. When I saw her, everything else faded. Terry had caught my interest, pulled me in with her stubbornness. But this woman was different. She felt...unspoiled. A rare thing in a place like this.

Terry became distant, her memory pushed back by the weight of this new discovery. This one was different. She was the spark I had been waiting for—the one who reignited that feeling I couldn't escape.

She drifted in and out of Goldie's on occasion, her visits infrequent and hesitant. She never fit in there—her beauty too refined, her demeanor too careful. It was as if she wandered through the grime, searching for something she couldn't name. Her presence unsettled the air around her, like she walked with purpose even if she didn't know where it led.

I watched her. She was always immaculately dressed, her clothes too polished for the grime-streaked sidewalks she wandered. I noted the way she moved—cautious but deliberate—the way her gaze flickered with a hint of fear when she passed certain faces. It wasn't just her appearance that set her apart; it was the way she navigated the filth, untouched by the desperation that clung to everyone else. It solidified my resolve. She wasn't just another face in the crowd. She was different. The pull I felt was immediate and unyielding.

Her name was Chelly. It burned itself into my mind, sharp and undeniable. She represented something the city had long since forgotten—an innocence that hadn't been swallowed whole. I needed her. Not for redemption. For something deeper. Something I couldn't name.

I followed her for days, learning her patterns, the rhythm of her movements. She always took the same path every night, slipping out of Goldie's and weaving through the side streets, her heels clicking softly against the pavement. There was something almost hypnotizing in the way she moved, like she was gliding through the world untouched by its grime. I trailed her steps with patience, waiting for the moment that felt right. When the skies broke open and rain began to fall, I knew it had come.

The downpour came sudden and unrelenting, washing over the city with a force that sent others scrambling for cover. But not her. She walked through it, head down, steps steady, as if the rain couldn't reach her. The streets thinned, people ducking into shops and doorways, leaving her alone under the downpour.

I approached her calmly, footsteps absorbed by the rain. She didn't notice me at first, too lost in her own thoughts. When I grabbed her from behind, she gasped—a sharp, brittle sound that fractured the stillness.

"Please," she stammered, voice cracking under the weight of panic. "I'll do anything… just don't hurt me."

I leaned in close, my voice steady and deliberate. "I'm here to save you."

Her body tensed, confusion running across her face. She didn't understand. How could she? None of them ever did.

The knife pressed forward, clean and deliberate. Her eyes widened, breath hitching as warmth spilled from the wound, spreading over my hands, thick and unyielding. Her body shuddered beneath my grip, life slipping away in trembling waves.

This was mercy. This was salvation. I murmured the scripture under my breath, words I had heard from my grandmother during long, echoing sermons: "And I will cleanse them from all their iniquity...and I will pardon all their sins."

The rain poured harder, washing the evidence away, thinning her blood as it ran along the pavement, carrying away the final traces of her existence. I watched it fade, absorbed by the storm.

They found her on September 6, 1990. By then, the rain had scrubbed the streets clean, leaving only her body—pale and still, eyes fixed on the sky as if searching for something she'd never find. They saw only death—never the salvation I had tried to gift her. The courts quietly attributed the act to him, another tally on a ledger already marked with his sins. He sat behind bars, cut off from the world, his name etched into their narrative.

But the city wasn't convinced. The newspapers questioned the convenience of it, the way the investigation had been neatly tied up despite the sketch they plastered across their front pages. It didn't match him. They knew it. The stories ran thinly veiled criticisms of the investigation, whispers of injustice laced between the lines.

But the police didn't care. They had their man. A Black body convicted was enough to call it justice. The sketch was quietly forgotten, filed away as coincidence, a mistake. Patrols thinned, investigations stalled. They had their answer, even if the city wasn't so sure.

And yet, I found myself wondering. The witness—the one who pointed the finger, who gave them the name that sealed his fate—had they seen me instead? I had been there, watching from the edges, close enough to be noticed. Close enough for the lines to blur.

I remember the way their descriptions changed in the papers—*tall, dark, dangerous.* I remember the sketch that never quite fit. But maybe it didn't need to. Maybe I could've stood beside him, and they wouldn't have seen the difference. To them, one Black man looked like another. The witness gave them a face, and the police made it fit. That was enough. A quick arrest, a name, a body behind bars. Headlines stopped screaming. The city breathed easier.

I moved through those same streets untouched, slipping back into the rhythm of the city without a single eye lingering too long. Patrols thinned, conversations drifted to other things, and the neighborhood settled back into its familiar grind. The police had moved on; so did the fear. But I watched. I listened. I waited, knowing the lull wouldn't last forever.

The nights grew longer, the air crisper, as the city braced itself for autumn's arrival. Leaves began to curl at the edges, whispering the promise of change. My grandparents spoke of gratitude and grace, their voices ringing with the hope only faith could provide. They planned for Thanksgiving with enthusiasm I couldn't match, their joy as hollow as the prayers they recited before every meal.

Thanksgiving came and went without fanfare. My grandparents busied themselves in the kitchen, fussing over dishes meant to feed a dozen but served to only three. The house filled with the familiar scent of roasted turkey and sweet potatoes, the air thick with cinnamon and sage. Plates were set meticulously, my grandmother smoothing each wrinkle from the tablecloth with hands that trembled slightly. Their conversations were laced with strained cheer, voices kept low as if silence alone could mend what was broken.

We sat around the table, forks scraping plates, the occasional clatter of a spoon the only disruption in the room. My grandfather cleared his throat, setting down his glass with deliberate care. His hands were thick with age, knuckles swollen, veins like rope beneath his skin. He looked at me, eyes narrowing slightly, and I could feel the weight of whatever he had been carrying pressing against his chest.

"You ever think about college, Derrick?" he asked, voice gravelly and worn. It wasn't a new question. He'd been asking it for months now, sometimes directly, sometimes couched in sermons about opportunity and the strength of education.

I glanced up from my plate, catching his gaze. "Sometimes," I replied, the lie sliding out easier than I'd expected. "I've been thinking about it more lately."

His eyes softened just a little, a flicker of hope sparking beneath the gray. "You're smart, boy. Smarter than most. I see you with them books, always writing. You got something there. It'd be a shame to waste it."

My grandmother nodded, her hands folded neatly in her lap. "Your stories are good, Derrick. Real good," she added, her voice fragile but earnest. "You always had a way with words."

I swallowed back the impulse to laugh. *Stories.* They had no idea what lived between those pages. The notebooks stacked beneath my bed, filled with thoughts that spilled out in the dead of night when I couldn't sleep. Observations. Reflections. Descriptions. They called it talent. I called it need.

"I'm just...thinking it over," I replied, pushing a piece of turkey around my plate. "I'm not sure what I want yet."

My grandfather's hand came down on the table with a gentleness I hadn't expected. "You got plenty of time, son. But think about it. Real hard. You got something in you. God doesn't give gifts for them to go unused."

The air felt heavier, stretched between expectation and resignation. I nodded, murmuring something vague and agreeable. But my mind was far from college applications and lecture halls. It was out there, roaming the streets, tracing familiar paths. It was back with her, in the rain, my hands slick and warm with purpose.

He watched me for a moment longer, like he could see something flickering just beneath the surface. "You don't want to get stuck," he said finally, voice dropping to a whisper only meant for me. "This world's got a way of keeping men in their place if they're not careful."

I met his gaze, unflinching. "I know."

The conversation drifted back to food, to the sermon planned for Sunday, to the neighbors and their squabbles. But my grandfather's words lingered, curling around my thoughts like smoke. He wanted more for me. He always had. But the path he saw for me was far different than the one I had already started carving out.

We cleared the plates, stacked them by the sink, and my grandmother wiped her hands on her apron, her movements soft and practiced. She touched my arm as I walked past, her fingers lingering for just a moment. "You do have a gift, Derrick," she said softly. "I hope you know that."

I nodded, offering her a smile I didn't feel. I know.

But she didn't. None of them did.

The house settled into its usual stillness, the echoes of their conversation fading into quiet prayers whispered behind closed doors. I crept back to my room, shutting the door behind me with a careful click. The notebooks were where I left them, stacked neatly beneath my bed, spines cracked and pages dog-eared from hours of restless scratching.

I pulled one out, its edges frayed from use, the pages heavy with inked confessions. My hands moved automatically, fingers trailing across familiar lines, descriptions of things I couldn't speak aloud. My grandfather's words still clung to me: God doesn't give gifts for them to go unused.

I almost laughed at the irony. A gift. That's what he called it. My mind drifted back to her—her eyes wide with fear, the rain washing the blood from my hands, streaking crimson into the gutters. I wondered if that's what it was: a gift. Something divine woven into my bones, urging me toward a purpose only I could see.

I lay back on the bed, the notebook still clutched in my hands, its pages splayed open like a confession. My eyes traced the lines I'd written, each stroke a testament to the pull I couldn't name, the craving that carved its place inside me long ago. Outside, the wind picked up, brushing leaves against the window like fingertips.

I closed my eyes, my grandfather's voice echoing through my mind. You don't want to get stuck. But I already was. I had been for years.

Sleep came slowly that night. It drifted in and out, teasing me with fragments of rest before pulling me back into the dark. His words clung to my thoughts, curling around my conscience like ivy, rooting themselves deeper with every breath. God doesn't give gifts for them to go unused.

I barely felt the pull of real sleep before the banging started—sharp, sudden, insistent. It shook me awake with a violence that left my chest tight and my skin prickling with dread. The first few hits rattled the walls, followed by muffled voices barking commands just beyond the door. I can still remember the rhythm of it, the way it reverberated through the house like some kind of cruel heartbeat.

Another round of pounding—urgent, brutal—fists against wood, then the creak of footsteps on the porch. Flashing red and blue lights seeped through the curtains, staining the darkness with frantic, swirling hues.

Sirens. Radios crackling. Boots crunching against gravel.

My heart lurched, adrenaline flooding my veins, sharp and electric. Panic clawed its way up my spine, sudden and fierce. I scrambled out of bed, nearly tripping over the heap of clothes I'd tossed aside the night before.
Had they found me? Had they finally traced everything back?

I can still feel the way the thought tightened around my throat, the way panic crashed against the inside of my ribs, tangled with something darker—an aching need to be seen. To be understood. To have my offerings unveiled for what they truly were. But I knew their judgment would be stained, their vision dulled by ignorance. They would taint my truth, smother it beneath their shallow perceptions.

The realization that I had grown reckless. Led by desire's fever, hunting with a desperation that left me exposed. Perhaps this was the moment they'd cast me into their light—but not like this. Never like this. Their broken gaze could never grasp the purity of my purpose. And still, part of me yearned for it—the recognition—even if it meant unraveling everything I had created.

What would they call me? A monster? A killer? Or would they see me as something more? Something necessary.

My hands shook as I braced myself against the dresser, fighting for breath. I felt exposed, cornered, the familiar need unraveling into raw desperation.

What did I miss? What did they find—a trail I thought I'd buried, evidence I'd left behind?

There was a part of me that almost felt relief. To stop running. To stop hiding behind the facade my grandparents so desperately clung to. But the craving still throbbed beneath my skin, clawing at my insides. It never stopped. It never let me rest.

I thought I was careful. That my precision kept me safe. But it didn't care for caution. It demanded more. And I had been too eager to feed it.

The knocking shattered my thoughts, too sudden, too real. Thuds like bone splintering, voices garbled and urgent, distorted by the distance but close enough to choke the air.

My grandfather's voice came to me, his voice heavy with scripture: "Woe unto them that seek deep to hide their counsel from the Lord, and their works are in the dark, and they say, Who seeth us? and who knoweth us?"

I hadn't understood it then—not fully. But now? What if nothing was hidden? What if they saw everything? From the start?

They know. That thought pierced me, sharp and gleaming. Was this how it would end? Unseen. Misunderstood. My work smothered beneath their blindness.

I needed them to understand. To see what I'd created. But not like this. Not in their hands, corrupted by ignorance.
Each beat of the knocking drove the thought deeper, splintering my resolve.

The urge to flee clawed at me, but something darker held me still. What if this was my unveiling? A reckoning they couldn't deny?

But I wasn't ready. Not yet. The air thickened, heavy with failure's acrid stench.

Another pounding, like a war drum calling out judgment, another command barked into the night. This time, the words found me.
"Open the door!"

I swallowed hard, my throat dry and raw. With each passing second, the urge to flee warred with the creeping acceptance that maybe this was what I deserved. Maybe they were right to come for me.

The verse echoed in my head, louder this time. "Woe unto them that seek deep to hide their counsel from the Lord." My body felt leaden, the weight of inevitability pressing down until movement itself became surrender.

The scripture clung to me, heavy and unforgiving. As if the darkness I embraced was never truly mine. As if I had simply been chosen to wield it.

I forced myself to move, legs stiff and unsteady as I stumbled toward the bedroom door. My hand hovered over the knob, fingers twitching.
One deep breath. Then another. My fingers

numbed, torn between surrender and defiance. And then, I turned the handle and stepped into the hallway, bracing myself for whatever judgment waited on the other side. Perhaps it was always meant to be. Perhaps the darkness I embraced was never mine to control, but merely a thread woven into something far greater. Let their judgment come.

I've written my gospel in blood.

And it has been absolute.

THOU SHALT SHOW UP

Thanksgiving Night, 1990

Verse: Psalm 51:1-12 (King James Version)

Have mercy upon me, O God, according to thy lovingkindness: according unto the multitude of thy tender mercies blot out my transgressions. Wash me thoroughly from mine iniquity, and cleanse me from my sin. For I acknowledge my transgressions: and my sin is ever before me. Against thee, thee only, have I

sinned, and done this evil in thy
sight: that thou mightest be
justified when thou speakest, and
be clear when thou judgest.
Behold, I was shapen in iniquity;
and in sin did my mother conceive
me. Behold, thou desirest truth in
the inward parts: and in the
hidden part thou shalt make me to
know wisdom. Purge me with
hyssop, and I shall be clean: wash
me, and I shall be whiter than
snow. Make me to hear joy and
gladness; that the bones which
thou hast broken may rejoice.
Hide thy face from my sins, and
blot out all mine iniquities. Create
in me a clean heart, O God; and
renew a right spirit within me.
Cast me not away from thy
presence; and take not thy holy
spirit from me. Restore unto me
the joy of thy salvation; and
uphold me with thy free spirit.

The prayer for redemption had surfaced as I
reached the doorknob, a scripture etched into my
memory from countless Sunday sermons. It had

never felt like it applied to me—not truly—not until this night.

I opened the door to the unknown. It felt inevitable—the pounding, the voices seeping through the frame. But instead of police, I saw my grandmother racing toward the main entrance, frantic and sobbing. She swung the door open, her voice strangled by sobs. "He's upstairs!" she wailed. "Please—help! He's not waking up!"

There were no police.

Behind her, the EMTs stormed through the doorway like soldiers breaching enemy lines. "Where is he?" one barked, urgency sharpening his tone.

"Upstairs," my grandmother cried, her shaking hand pointing toward the staircase. "He's in the bedroom." Her voice cracked, splintering into a thousand desperate fragments.

I stood there, frozen in the hallway. My body wouldn't move, wouldn't breathe. The EMTs rushed past me, their footsteps a stampede of urgency. The creak of the stairs groaned under their weight, their voices echoing back down to me.

My grandmother rushed to me and threw her arms around me, clutching me like a lifeline. Her sobs raked against my chest; a sensation so foreign I almost didn't recognize it. Warmth. Comfort. I wondered if this was what it was supposed to feel like.

When I finally moved, it was as if I had been yanked forward by an invisible string. We followed; my grandmother's frail fingers still wrapped around my arm. The bedroom door was open, light spilling out into the darkened hallway. I couldn't see his face, only the blur of hands working—pushing, pressing, pleading with his chest to rise.

"Come on," one of them said, voice taut with urgency. "Come on, damn it."

They cut away his shirt, revealing lifeless skin. They placed adhesive pads on his chest and shoulders, connecting them to a machine I didn't recognize. CPR, chest compressions, breaths forced into his lungs. They counted aloud, a mechanical litany against the silence.

But nothing changed.

One of them shook his head, his expression

hardening into resignation. "Time of death..." he murmured, glancing at his watch.

The words hit me like ice, cold and merciless. My grandfather was gone. No violence. No blood. Just stillness. A clean death, untarnished by the filth I had come to know so well.

I felt my grandmother crumble beside me, her knees buckling as if the world had been ripped out from beneath her. I held her up. I had to. Because now, she only had me.

And somehow, that terrified me more than anything else.

I stayed there long after the EMTs left. After they zipped up the black bag. After the gurney wheels stopped squeaking. After the stillness returned like a fog that clung to the walls and filled the spaces between every breath.

I sat at the foot of the bed, staring at the impression where his body had just been.

The first time I saw death stripped of chaos, it was his. No crimson stains pooling beneath broken bodies, no screams clawing at the air, no shadows lurking in the corners of my mind. Just stillness. Absence. And for the first time, I grieved. Not for myself. Not even for my grandmother. But for him.

He didn't deserve this kind of ending—alone and unconscious, his body surrendering while we slept. It seemed cruel, almost indifferent, the way life could just seep out of a person without fanfare or violence. I had seen life ripped away before, felt it drain beneath my hands, heard its last desperate gasp. But this was different. This was quiet. And that silence pressed against my ears like a weight I couldn't shake.

He was the only person who ever believed I could be anything more than what the streets tried to shape me into. The only man who saw a future for me beyond cracked sidewalks and shattered glass. He taught me how to tie a tie, how to shake a man's hand with confidence and look him in the eye, even to be honest if the truth hurt. He would read my poems like they mattered, marking them up with his worn-out pen, nodding with that quiet pride that didn't need words. He said I had a gift.

I didn't understand it then. Not fully. I couldn't see what he saw. But I do now. I saw it in the way his hands had stilled, the way his chest lay unmoving under the sterile light of the EMTs. I saw it in the emptiness that had settled over his room, the indent on the mattress where he used to sleep, the slippers he left by the door as if he'd just stepped out for a moment. I saw it in the way my grandmother's voice broke when she called his name long after the EMTs had left, as if saying it enough times would bring him back.

The funeral was quiet. The church was packed tighter than I'd expected, the pews brimming with faces I barely recognized—old neighbors, distant family members, men in worn suits with their hats pressed to their chests. My grandmother clung to my arm as we walked down the aisle, her fingers curled around mine, squeezing every few steps as if to remind herself I was still there.

The scent of lilies hung heavy in the air, mixing with the stale undertone of old wood and candle wax. My grandfather's casket rested at the front, draped in white cloth and flanked by towering arrangements of flowers that seemed almost too bright for the occasion. His photograph sat on a small table beside it, framed and polished. It was him before the sickness took its toll—strong, upright, his eyes holding that familiar gleam of stubbornness that I'd inherited.

We took our seats near the front, and I kept my eyes on the floor, tracing the worn patterns in the carpet while voices around me hummed low and mournful. The pastor spoke first, his voice solemn but steady, recounting my grandfather's years of service to the community, his time in the Navy, his faith that never wavered. I listened, but the words barely touched me. They felt distant, almost rehearsed.

It wasn't until they opened the floor for anyone who wanted to speak that the room seemed to change. People rose one by one, some clutching tissues, others simply staring straight ahead as they spoke. Stories spilled out—how my grandfather fixed roofs without asking for a dime, how he brought groceries to the elderly on our block, how he used to sit on his porch and wave to every car that passed by, as if each one carried someone worth knowing.

When it was my turn, I hadn't planned on standing. But my grandmother nudged me, her eyes red-rimmed and pleading. I swallowed hard and rose to my feet, the eyes of the room turning toward me with a weight I could almost feel pressing against my chest. My hand shook as I pulled the folded paper from my jacket pocket, smoothing it out with careful fingers. I had written it the night before—scratched it out in the dark with only the glow of the streetlight slipping through my window.

I cleared my throat, the sound breaking the stillness, and I began:

"The Weight of Your Hands

You taught me that hands weren't just for fighting—
They were bridges, binding fractured worlds,
Strong enough to hold a heart that's breaking,
Soft enough to cradle dreams unfurled.

You showed me that calluses were maps,
Etched with years of toil and sacrifice,
That strength was not in what you could carry alone,
But in the burdens you chose to lift for others' lives.

Patience, you said, wasn't surrender,
It was faith with its sleeves rolled high,
That forgiveness wasn't erasing the hurt,
But building a place where pain could die.

I watched you fix what others would discard,
Hands steady, eyes calm like rivers at dawn,
You didn't need words to tell me you loved me—
I felt it in the grip of your palms.

When storms came, you were my unyielding anchor,
A lighthouse standing tall against the waves,
You held the line when I drifted too far,
Calling me back to the path you paved.

The words wavered in the air, and I forced myself to continue:

Now you're gone, and the world feels heavier,
The weight of all you carried is mine to bear,
I press my hands to the earth and whisper,
I will lift what you left, I swear.

Because love, you taught me, isn't always loud,
Sometimes it's the silence of two hands clasped,
The steady hum of presence when words are brittle,
The breath shared when the world collapses.

I'm learning to build with these hands you raised,
To mend what's broken, to hold what's frayed,
And though you're gone, your fingerprints remain—
I see them in the strength I've made.

For you taught me that love didn't need to be spoken,
It lived in the doing, in each tender repair,
In the way you sat beside me, still and whole,
Reminding me that love is always there."

When the casket began its slow descent, something inside me sank with it—an anchor slipping into depths I couldn't reach. I couldn't name it, but I felt it give way—heavy and unrelenting, pulling me down with a force that left me breathless. My grandmother's grip slackened, her hand dropping to her side, weighted by grief too dense to hold. Her knees buckled, collapsing as if the ground itself had given out beneath her. I caught her before she fell completely, holding her upright as she sobbed into my chest, her weight pressing into me like she was sinking too, dragged under by the gravity of goodbye.

I held her there, feeling the rain seep through my clothes, watching the dirt fall in clumps over the polished wood. And I made a promise—not to God, not even to my grandmother—but to him. To the memory of the man who taught me what strength could look like when it wasn't masked by violence. He always believed I could be more, that there was still light in me worth fighting for. I would make him proud. Somehow, I would.

But the truth is, I didn't know how. Redemption was a concept I couldn't hold in my hands; it was smoke and prayer, something reserved for church pews and whispered confessions. I wasn't even sure I deserved it. But I knew I owed him something. I owed him proof that his faith in me wasn't a mistake. That the way he saw me was real, even if I couldn't see it myself.

I remember going through his things a few days after the funeral, the house still heavy with the smell of sympathy and lilies. Grandma couldn't bring herself to touch anything yet. His shoes were still by the door, polished and waiting. His ties hung neatly on the rack, knotted just the way he'd taught me. I took the one he always wore to church—a dark maroon with a thin silver stripe—and slipped it into my pocket. It felt like something sacred. I'd never been good at goodbyes.

"He was proud of you, you know." Grandma's voice startled me. I hadn't even heard her come in. She leaned against the doorway, her hand pressed to her chest like she was holding something inside. "He always told me you were too smart for this city. That you'd be the one to get out." She smiled, though it didn't reach her eyes. "He used to mark up those poems of yours. Said you had a way with words."

I nodded, feeling something tighten in my throat. I hadn't written anything since he died. Couldn't bring myself to. It felt like an intrusion—like picking up the pen would mean he was really gone.

"You gonna keep writing?" she asked, her eyes searching mine.

I didn't answer. I didn't have one. But I slipped that tie into my back pocket and held on to it like a promise—an unspoken vow that tethered me to something beyond the streets, beyond the stain of my own hands. I wasn't sure what it meant yet. I wasn't sure of anything. But I knew I owed him something. His belief in me had been unyielding, even when mine faltered. And maybe words were all I had left to give. Maybe they were the only offering that didn't come with a cost.

The days that followed were heavy with stillness. My grandmother moved through the house like she was waiting for someone to turn the lights back on, her eyes dim with grief. I tried to help where I could—cleaning dishes, taking out the trash, holding her steady when her legs trembled under the weight of loss. But I was just as lost as she was. I wandered the house at night, trailing my fingers along the walls he had built, the furniture he had polished. His scent still lingered in the hallway, a faint trace of tobacco and aftershave that refused to fade.

It was during one of those mornings—her voice cracking as she suggested we look at smaller places—that I realized I couldn't just drift through these halls forever. I couldn't be another ghost haunting these walls, trailing regret behind me like smoke. But the talk of moving—it lingered, unspoken but always there, curling around the breakfast table like a fog neither of us could see through.

One morning, the tension finally broke. She was sitting at the kitchen table, a cup of tea cradled in her hands. The newspaper was spread out in front of her, the classified section folded open. Circles were drawn around addresses I didn't recognize, little stars scribbled in the margins.

"You're looking again?" I asked, though I already knew the answer.

She nodded, her gaze fixed on a listing. "This one's not too far from here. Little two-bedroom...small yard...less to clean," she said, her voice drifting off like she couldn't quite finish the thought. She set the paper down, smoothing the wrinkles with her palms. "It's just too much, baby. This house...I can't keep up with it alone. And the bills..." She shook her head. "They're stacking up. I don't know how much longer I can—"

Her voice broke, and she covered her mouth with her hand. I'd never seen her cry—not like this. Not quietly. It was always a burst, a storm that came and left just as fast. But this was different. This was something heavy, something that wouldn't leave with the morning light.

"Grandma," I started, pulling out the chair across from her. "We don't have to move. I'll figure something out. I'll pick up more hours at the shop, I can—"

She cut me off with a sad smile, her eyes still wet. "You're not working yourself to the bone just so I can hold on to something that ain't ours to keep." She gestured around the room, her hands shaking. "It's too much. The heating, the roof that leaks, the taxes... It's all too much."

I looked around, really looked this time. The chipped paint on the window sills, the fraying edges of the carpet, the stack of unopened bills on the counter. She was right. It was too much. My grandfather had always handled the finances—

had a way of making things stretch further than they should. But without him, everything was unraveling.

"You shouldn't have to carry this alone," I said finally, my voice barely above a whisper.

Her eyes softened. "And neither should you."

We sat in silence, the weight of the room pressing down on us. I reached across the table and took her hand, her skin thin and papery beneath my grip. "I'm going to help. We'll find something. Together."

She squeezed my hand, the strength in her grip surprising. "I know you will." Her voice cracked just a little. "I just want you to be happy, baby. I want you to have more than this."

I swallowed hard, the truth scraping against my throat. "I'll figure it out. I promise."

Her eyes lingered on mine for a moment, searching for something I wasn't sure I could give. But she nodded, and that was enough. She slid the newspaper across the table, the circles and stars glaring up at me like wounds. "I called a few places. Maybe you can go check them out? I don't drive much anymore..."

"I got it," I said, standing up and folding the paper neatly. "I'll go today."

Her smile was small but real. "You're a good boy," she whispered. "Always have been."

I almost flinched at that. But I just nodded, clutching the paper like a lifeline. "I'll be back by dinner."

The walk to the bus stop was slow, each step dragging with the weight of decisions I hadn't been ready to make. I clutched the classifieds in my hand, scanning the addresses, tracing the numbers with my thumb. I'd never house-hunted before, didn't even know what to look for. But I knew one thing—she wouldn't have to carry this weight alone. Not anymore.

And as I waited for the bus, the paper crumpled in my hands, I thought of him. Of the way he'd fix things without a word, his hands steady and sure. He'd have known what to do. He always did. I slipped my hand into my pocket, fingers brushing against the frayed edge of his tie. I pulled it out, held it up to the morning light. It was still there, still holding its shape despite everything.

I didn't have his hands. I didn't have his strength. But I had his faith. And that would have to be enough.

I got back home just before dinner, the paper folded neatly under my arm. My grandmother had already set the table, two plates positioned across from each other like they always had been. She didn't ask about the listings, and I didn't offer. We ate in silence, the clatter of forks and the scrape of chairs the only sound between us. When I stood to clear the plates, she touched my arm—lightly, like she wasn't sure if she had the right.

"Did you find anything worth seeing?" she asked, her voice soft and steady.

I nodded, though I wasn't sure if it was the truth. "A couple of places. I'll go back tomorrow, check them out."

She smiled—a sad, grateful smile that I could feel in my chest. "You're a good boy," she said again, and this time I didn't flinch.

That night, I sat at the kitchen table long after she went to bed. The classifieds were spread out before me, but my eyes drifted to the pamphlet that had been buried beneath them. Community College of Philadelphia—Build Your Future. I didn't even remember picking it up. Maybe I grabbed it on instinct, like my hands had moved before my mind caught up. I traced the edge of the paper, my fingers brushing over the words English Major.

I thought about him—my grandfather. The way he'd read my poems, marking them up with his old ballpoint pen, nodding along with that silent approval that never needed to be spoken. He'd tell me to use my voice, to make them listen. I never understood what he meant back then. But sitting at that kitchen table, the house too quiet, the light above me flickering against the ceiling, I wondered if maybe I did now.

The next morning, I told my grandmother I was going out to check on the listings. She didn't ask where, just nodded and handed me a container of leftovers. "You'll get hungry," she said, pressing it into my hands like a ritual. I kissed her cheek and left, the pamphlet tucked inside my jacket.

The bus ride to Community College wasn't long, but it felt like miles. I sat near the window, watching the city pass by in blurs of gray and rust. The buildings stood like tired sentinels, graffiti and grime marking their surfaces. I wondered how many stories were buried behind those walls, how many ghosts lingered in the alleyways. It was different when you weren't looking for them.

When the bus lurched to a stop, I stepped off and stared up at the campus. It wasn't much—just tired bricks and narrow windows, lines of students moving in clusters. A few walked alone, earbuds shoved in, eyes fixed forward. But there was a rhythm to it, a pulse that made me pause. I wasn't used to seeing movement that didn't have desperation tied to it.

I made my way to the admissions office, my footsteps heavier than I intended. The door creaked when I opened it, and the woman behind the desk glanced up, her smile polite and practiced.

"Can I help you?" she asked, her fingers still tapping at the keyboard.

I nodded, clearing my throat. "I...I wanted to ask about registering. For classes."

Her smile brightened, and she straightened in her chair. "Of course! Are you looking for this semester or the spring?"

I hadn't thought that far ahead. I stared at her, then down at my hands. "As soon as I can."

She nodded, turning to grab a stack of papers from the file drawer. "You'll need to fill out an application. And we'll need transcripts if you have them. Are you looking for full-time or part-time?"

I hesitated. I hadn't considered that either. "Full-time, I think."

Her eyes softened, and she slid the paperwork across the counter. "Take your time. Fill these out, and we'll get you started."

I took the forms and found a chair by the window, the pamphlet still folded in my back pocket. I ran my fingers over the lines, my handwriting slow and deliberate. Name. Address. Social Security. It all felt too normal, too routine for the path I'd carved out for myself. But I wrote anyway, each letter a promise I wasn't sure I could keep.

The last section asked for a major, and I stared at it for a long time. The pen hovered above the paper, my hand trembling just slightly. I closed my eyes, the image of my grandfather flashing behind my eyelids—him at the kitchen table, his glasses perched on his nose, a stack of my poems in his hands. You got a gift, boy, he used to say. Ain't nobody can take that from you.

When I opened my eyes, I wrote it down. English.

I handed the papers back to the woman at the desk, and she looked them over with quick, practiced eyes. "Looks good. You'll get a letter in the mail about your start date and your schedule."

"Thank you," I murmured, shoving my hands in my pockets.

She smiled again. "You're welcome. Good luck."

I stepped back out into the cold, the door swinging shut behind me. The campus moved around me—students laughing, some huddled over books, others leaning against the walls like they owned the place. I slipped the pamphlet back into my pocket and walked away, my footsteps steady and sure.

I didn't know what I was doing. I didn't know if I belonged. But I had shown up. And maybe, just maybe, that was enough.

Looking back, I think that walk across campus was the first time I'd ever really chosen something. Not inherited it. Not survived it. But chosen it. The city had always dictated my path—its pulse thrumming beneath my feet, whispering its demands in every broken streetlight, every siren scream that sliced through the night. But this—this was different. I wasn't running from something. I was walking toward it.

My grandfather used to say that education was the one thing they couldn't take from you. "They can take your money, your pride, hell—even your life," he'd say, a cigarette dangling from his lips, "but what you learn...that's yours." He never made it past the tenth grade, but he spoke like a man who'd written his own scripture. I think maybe he had.

I didn't walk away from that campus that day with hope—not exactly. Hope was still a language I didn't understand, a tongue too foreign to form. But I did leave with something else. Something quieter. A flicker of resolve that didn't require belief, just action. I didn't know if I could be saved. I didn't know if redemption was something you could earn or if it had to be given. But I knew I could try. And maybe that was enough.

And maybe, just maybe, it was the first step toward becoming something more than I had been.

And it kept me close to Grandma, too. Maybe we could keep the house they worked so hard for; I don't think she had the strength to move. She was already starting to change. Slower in the mornings. Shaky on the stairs. Her voice would trail off mid-sentence, her eyes scanning corners of the room like they held pieces of something she was trying to remember. She needed me. That much was clear. And I needed to be better. Stronger.

So I stayed.

But the hunger didn't leave. If anything, it only grew quieter. Smarter. It wrapped itself around my good intentions, hissing in the back of my mind that I was pretending. That I was wearing my grandfather's decency like a mask. That eventually, I would rip it off and return to who I really was.

And maybe I would have, if not for that Thursday night in church.

I wasn't even supposed to be there. The service had ended over an hour ago, and I had stayed behind to help fold bulletins for Sunday. Grandma liked me near the pulpit lately, said it gave her peace. I did it for her, but truth be told, I liked the quiet. The hush of the sanctuary, the scent of wood polish and candle wax—it felt like I could hear myself think in there. Like maybe God was still willing to listen.

The overhead lights had been dimmed, leaving soft shadows to settle in the pews. A few candles still glinted near the altar, their glow dancing across the crimson cloth draped over the pulpit. The choir loft above was empty, but I swore I could still hear the echo of their last hymn, a lingering hum in the silence.

I walked slowly down the center aisle, the hush inside the sanctuary wrapping around me like a warm quilt against the cold ache of everything I couldn't name. Each step echoed softly on the tile floor. The stained-glass windows, dim in the evening light, cast fractured reds and blues across the walls, like the last traces of grace stretching to reach me.

I paused by the altar, running my hand across the velvet cloth. I closed my eyes and listened. No voices. No cries. Just the settling creak of old beams and the quiet, steady rhythm of breath in my chest. For a moment, I wasn't haunted. I wasn't a shadow with blood beneath my nails. I was just a grandson. A man who missed the only father figure he'd ever known.

I rested my hands on my knees and looked up at the cross above the pulpit.

"If you're there," I whispered, "just... help me stay."

That was it. No rehearsed prayer. No bargain. Just a whisper.

So I stood. Not expecting a sign. Not expecting anything.

But something was waiting for me.

I wandered toward the back, trailing my fingers along the edge of the pews. That's when I saw the flyer.

It was crooked, taped to the corkboard just outside the fellowship hall.

"Struggling with addiction? You're not alone. Thursdays at 7PM. All are welcome."

I stared at it for a long time. Not because of what it said, but because of what it didn't. It didn't say what you had to be addicted to. Just that you were welcome. Just that you could speak. Be heard. Be seen.

And in that moment, I realized I wasn't looking for forgiveness.

I was looking for something to keep me from falling.

And maybe—just maybe—I had found it.

He would've told me this was a start. That maybe staying wasn't about running from who I was, but choosing who I could become.

The church basement smelled like old coffee and

despair. Folding chairs were arranged in a rough circle, some occupied, some waiting. Fluorescent lights buzzed overhead, flickering in places, casting long shadows across the linoleum floor.

I kept to the back at first, unsure if I belonged. Everyone looked different, but the weight they carried felt familiar—grief, shame, longing. Some clutched coffee cups like lifelines, others stared at the floor, waiting for the meeting to start.

A woman with soft eyes and a clipboard offered me a small smile. "You're welcome here," she said, her voice warm but not invasive.

I nodded, not trusting my voice just yet, and took a seat along the edge of the circle. No one stared. No one judged. They just waited.

The meeting began with a reading.

"God, grant me the serenity to accept the things I cannot change, Courage to change the things I can, And wisdom to know the difference. Living one day at a time; Enjoying one moment at a time; Accepting hardship as a pathway to peace; Taking, as He did, this sinful world as it is, not as I would have it; Trusting that He will make all things right if I surrender to His Will; That I may be reasonably happy in this life and supremely happy with Him forever in the next. Amen."

Then came silence.

And then someone spoke.

A man in his forties with sunken cheeks and a crushed cup in his hands leaned forward, elbows on his knees, his voice low and uneven. "I used to wake up every day thinking it would be different. That I'd get clean, get right, just... stop. But it's like trying to hold water in your hands. No matter how tight you grip, it slips right through. I lost my job. My wife left. Took my daughter. And I don't blame her. I was chasing something that kept hollowing me out, and I still couldn't stop."

He paused, staring into the bottom of his cup as if the answers might be there.

"I don't know if I'll ever get it back. I don't even know what 'it' is anymore. But I'm here. I'm trying. That's all I've got."

He didn't name it. He didn't have to.

I listened, heart pounding. My addiction didn't come in a bottle or a needle. Mine was buried deep beneath my skin, silent and coiled like a serpent. But still, his words found me.

One by one, others followed. Some shared victories. Others confessed failures. But all of them—every single one—were trying.

And for the first time in my life, I didn't feel alone.

When it came time for introductions, I hesitated. My lips parted, but the words stuck in my throat. I wasn't ready to speak. Not yet.

But I stayed.

And in the corner of the room, sitting across from me, was a woman who didn't speak either. Her eyes were dark and steady, her posture calm but guarded. She looked at me—not through me— and for a flicker of a second, I felt seen.

Later, she spoke. Her voice was soft but certain, with a steadiness earned through struggle.

"My name's Camille," she said. "And as of today, I have four years, three months, and ten days sober."

The room responded with nods, murmurs of support. She smiled, but it didn't quite reach her eyes.

"I count every single day because every day matters. Some days it's easy. Most days, it's not. But I take it one at a time. Because that's all any of us can do."

She looked around the room, then down at her hands.

"I lost everything. My dignity. My family. My faith. But I didn't lose myself—not completely. And when I walked into this room four years ago, I found strength."

Her gaze lifted and, for the briefest moment, met mine again.

"If you're here, then you're already doing the hardest part. You showed up."

I didn't know what to call the feeling her words gave me. It wasn't relief. It wasn't peace. It was the ache of possibility. Of something shifting, deep inside, where no one else could see.

I didn't know her.

But I would.

The meeting began to wind down. A few more people shared, voices low and raw, weaving their own confessions into the fabric of the room. Pain and hope, shame and strength—it all mixed together into something almost holy.

Then came the close.

The group stood in a circle, hands reaching out, some touching, some hovering.

A voice led the way: "God, grant me the serenity to accept the things I cannot change, courage to change the things I can, and wisdom to know the difference."

We echoed the words together, and when it ended, another voice followed:

"God's will, not mine, be done."

A chorus of voices replied: "Keep coming back. It works if you work it."

And just like that, it was over.

But something in me had shifted. Maybe just a little. Maybe just enough.

I lingered, unsure if I should be the first to leave. The others filtered out with soft nods and half-smiles, but I stayed rooted to the floor, staring at the empty chairs as if they still held echoes of everything I had just heard.

That's when I saw her again.

Camille.

She approached with a paper cup in her hand and a gentleness that didn't feel forced.

"You did good just being here," she said.

I nodded. "I wasn't sure I belonged."

"That's the thing," she said. "You don't have to be sure. You just have to show up."

She glanced around the room, then added, "If you keep coming, you might want to find a sponsor — someone who's been through it, who can help you when things get heavy."

I looked at her, curiosity rising. "A sponsor?"

She smiled, a little wry. "Think of it like a guide. Someone who knows the path, even when it's dark. You don't have to do this alone."

I paused, the question forming in my chest before I could stop it. "Would you ever…?"

Her smile deepened, a touch bittersweet. She shook her head gently. "I'm flattered. But I'm not ready to be that for anyone. Not yet."

She looked me in the eye, her voice soft but certain. "But I'll see you here next Thursday. Same time."

I wanted to say something—anything—but all I could do was nod.

She turned and walked toward the door, and I watched her go. Something about her presence lingered long after she was gone.

Maybe this was what beginning again felt like. Not fireworks. Not certainty. Just the quiet promise of showing up.

I walked home in silence.

The streets were slick from a recent rain, shining beneath the streetlights like glass shattered across the pavement. I shoved my hands in my pockets, not to warm them, but to keep them still. The same hands that had taken lives now trembled from a conversation.

Camille's voice replayed in my head, softer than the wind, louder than my thoughts: You don't have to be sure. You just have to show up.

Was that what this was? Showing up? Was that enough to count as change?

The house was dark when I stepped inside.

My grandmother had already gone to bed, the TV left on low in the living room. The static glow danced across the floorboards. I sat on the edge of the couch, stared at the blank screen. My grandfather's old slippers were still beside his recliner.

I imagined what he might've said if he'd seen me walk through the doors of that church. Maybe he would've cried. Maybe he would've prayed. Maybe he would've simply nodded and said, "Took you long enough, boy."

I wanted to believe he'd be proud.

That night, I didn't dream about blood. I didn't dream at all.

Only silence.

And for the first time in a long while, I didn't hate it.

The next morning came without fanfare—just sunlight bleeding through the blinds and the familiar clink of dishes from the kitchen.

I moved slowly, dragging my feet toward the smell of coffee and something frying on the stove. My grandmother stood with her back to me, wrapped in one of my grandfather's old robes. It hung off her small frame like a memory too big to wear.

"You stayed late after church last night," she said without turning around.

I froze, halfway to the fridge. "Yeah."

She glanced over her shoulder. "You alright?"

I hesitated. It would've been easy to say yes and leave it at that. But something in her tone—or maybe in the quiet of the house without him—made me want to tell the truth.

"There was a meeting. In the basement," I said.

"For people dealing with addiction."

She didn't say anything at first, just nodded slowly, as if waiting for the rest.

"I didn't plan on going," I added. "I was just curious. Thought I'd peek in and leave."

"And?" she asked gently, setting the spatula down.

"I stayed."

"Why?"

"I think..." I swallowed, unsure how to put it into words. "I think I stayed because I needed to understand. Her. My mom. What she went through. What she gave into."

Her eyes softened.

"And maybe," I continued, "maybe it'll help me grieve him too. Pop. I don't know. I just... I don't want to carry this the way I've been carrying it."

She walked over and placed a hand on my cheek. "Whatever it takes to heal, baby. You try it. Don't let anyone make you feel less for needing something."

I nodded, emotion swelling in my throat. She squeezed my hand and turned back to the stove.

"I made you eggs. You've got a first day to get ready for."

Her words landed soft, but something in me flinched. Not from the gesture—never that—but from the unfamiliar weight of being cared for. It was a kindness I hadn't earned, yet it wrapped around me like the smell of breakfast and memory. I nodded, whispering a quiet thank you, though I wasn't sure she heard me over the hiss of the skillet."

We ate quietly, each lost in thought. Her eyes lingered on me a few times, like she was memorizing the shape of my shoulders, the tiredness in my face, the quiet resolve behind my gaze. Maybe she was afraid I'd vanish next, like him. Or maybe she just saw something unfamiliar in me.

After breakfast, I went back to my room and opened the notebook I hadn't touched since his funeral.

Not for class. Just to write.

Diary Entry – November 1991

It's strange how quickly routine sets in. The bell chimes at eight. The lectures spill out in waves — syntax, structure, Baldwin, Morrison. Names that felt like ghosts on the page now linger in the back of my mind, shaping thoughts I never knew I could hold. I still sit in the back, still keep my head down, but I listen. I listen to the way words can bend, the way sentences can be stacked like bricks, building something out of nothing. Maybe that's what I'm doing. Building.

I can't help but think of him sometimes. My grandfather. His hands thick with callouses, fingers stained with oil from fixing cars that weren't even his. He used to say that learning was like laying bricks. One word at a time, one sentence, one idea stacked on top of another. "Build your mind like a fortress," he'd say, "and the world can't tear it down." I don't know if he believed that or if he just wanted me to, but I hold on to it. Because I need to.

I'm learning how to be patient. How to listen without speaking. How to write without bleeding. The professors are kind, mostly. Some of them look at me like I'm a stranger; others nod with that soft kind of respect reserved for the quiet ones. I don't mind it. I don't need to be seen. I just need to keep moving forward.

And then there's Camille.

I didn't plan on meeting her, much less seeing her week after week. But the group became a kind of rhythm—every Thursday at 7 p.m. A room full of people looking for redemption, for something to hold onto. I guess I was one of them. Camille was too.

She's different. The way she speaks—it's not like the others. Her voice carries weight, like each word has been carved out of stone. She talks about struggle like it's something sacred, something that purifies you if you can survive it. I listen when she speaks. Really listen. Because she talks about the kind of hope I didn't think existed, the kind that doesn't need proof, just faith.

Last week she shared something that's stuck with me. "I used to think addiction was the chain," she said, eyes steady and unflinching. "But it's not. The chain is the reason you reach for it." She let that hang in the air, and I felt it settle into my bones. I still feel it.

Nearly a year and I still don't talk much during the meetings. I watch. I listen. But she notices me. Sometimes she'll catch my eye and nod like she knows something I haven't figured out yet. It's unsettling. It's also the only time I feel real.

> I still don't know what I'm
> building. A life, maybe. A chance.
> Or maybe it's just an illusion I'm
> stacking brick by brick, hoping it
> doesn't collapse. But it's
> something. And right now, that's
> enough.

I don't remember how it happened exactly. One moment, we were just two strangers sitting in folding chairs, listening to confessions spill from weary mouths like prayers that no one would ever answer. And then, we were something else. I still can't tell you what that something is—not fully. But I know it started the night she asked me to walk her home.

It was late, the November air brittle and sharp, biting through our coats as we stepped out of the church basement. I'd gotten used to walking back alone, the silence wrapping around me like a cloak, but that night was different. Camille lingered at the door, her hands shoved deep into her pockets, eyes fixed on the cracked concrete beneath her feet.

"You mind?" she asked, her voice softer than I'd ever heard it.

"Mind what?"

"Walking with me."

I should've said no. I should've turned away and let her walk alone. I'd never been good at proximity—closeness led to questions, questions led to suspicion, and suspicion cracked the surface of the lies I'd wrapped myself in. But there she was, standing in the doorway with the kind of hope that's impossible to ignore. So I nodded, and we fell into step, two shadows stretching long beneath the streetlights.

For a while, neither of us spoke. The city stretched out around us, its bones creaking beneath the weight of its own sickness, but beside her, it felt...different. Lighter, somehow. I'd never thought about the city that way before. I'd only ever seen it as something that needed to be purged, cleansed of its filth. But walking with her, I found myself watching the way her breath fogged the air, how her footsteps fell into rhythm with mine. It was like she belonged here—like she was meant to carve out a piece of this place and call it hers.

She broke the silence first. "You been coming to the meetings long?"

"Not really," I replied. "When I met you was my first one."

She nodded, her eyes still fixed on the pavement ahead. "It helps. I mean...it can help. If you let it."

I didn't say anything. I wasn't sure I believed her. But I liked the way she said it, the way she spoke like she knew what it meant to try and fail and try again.

We walked a few more blocks, our breaths mingling in the cold. When her building came into view, she slowed her pace, almost reluctant. I felt it too—that tug at the end of something good, the kind of thing you're not sure you're ready to let go of.

"Do you...you wanna come up?" she asked, her voice barely above a whisper.

I hesitated. Everything in me screamed to say no. I wasn't ready for this. I wasn't built for this. But there she was, looking at me with that same kind of hope she'd held at the door, and I couldn't turn away. So I nodded, and she smiled. A real smile, not the kind you fake to keep people from asking questions.

Her apartment was small, cluttered with books and mismatched furniture, the kind of place that felt lived in. Safe. She shrugged off her coat and tossed it onto the arm of the couch. "You want coffee?"

"Sure."

I moved toward the bookshelves, my fingers tracing the spines. Baldwin. Angelou. Hemingway. Names I recognized. Names my grandfather had mentioned once or twice. I pulled one from the shelf—*Go Tell It on the Mountain*. The pages were worn, the corners dog-eared and soft. I thumbed through it, letting the scent of old paper settle into my lungs.

"That one's my favorite," she said from the doorway, a mug of coffee in each hand.

"Yeah?"

She nodded, setting the mugs down on the coffee table. "It's real. Honest."

I slipped it back onto the shelf and joined her on the couch, the springs groaning beneath our weight. She handed me the mug, her fingers brushing mine for just a second—long enough for me to notice, long enough for me to wonder if she'd done it on purpose.

We sat on her worn-out couch, sipping coffee that was too strong but somehow perfect. She talked about the meetings—how they'd saved her life, how she'd spent two years clawing her way back from the edge. I listened, really listened, and it wasn't until she stopped speaking that I realized I hadn't thought about the darkness in hours. Not once.

"Why'd you come?" she asked suddenly, her eyes steady on mine.

"To the meetings?"

She nodded.

I hesitated. I could've lied. I probably should have. But there was something in her gaze that made me want to be honest. "I needed to understand."

"Understand what?"

I took a breath. "My mother. And...myself."

Her expression softened, and for a moment, I thought she was going to press further, but she didn't. She just nodded, like she understood exactly what I meant.

We sat there, the silence stretching out between us, but it didn't feel heavy. It felt like it mattered.

"I'm glad you came," she said finally, her voice so soft I almost didn't hear it.

"Me too," I replied, and I meant it.

We talked for hours after that—about things that didn't matter and things that did. She told me about her family, her sister she hadn't spoken to in years, the way she still dreamt of her father's old record player humming softly in the background of her childhood. I told her about my grandmother, the way she still left the back door open for stray cats, how she always said prayers over her coffee before she took a sip.

Camille laughed at that, not out of mockery but with something like admiration. "That's beautiful," she said, her eyes shining. "To believe in something that much."

I nodded, feeling something shift inside me—something I didn't have a name for.

I didn't want to leave that night. I didn't want to walk back into the city alone, back into the chaos that waited for me. But I stood, slipping my coat back over my shoulders. She walked me to the door, her hand lingering on the frame.

"You coming back to the meeting next week?" she asked.

"Yeah," I replied, my voice firmer than I expected. "I'll be there."

She smiled, that same real smile from before, and I felt it—hope, sprouting up through the fractured places I thought would never heal. I wanted to call it love, but that felt too simple, too easy. Love was like a weed. It didn't need roots to grow—it just took hold wherever it landed, clawing its way through stone and shadow, surviving on the barest scraps of light. I had seen it before—love without roots, blooming in the most broken places. It could exist without promise, without permanence, feeding off desperation.

But this…this was something else.

With her, I felt grounded. Safe. She made me feel heard in a way I hadn't known I needed. Safety was different from love. It needed roots—deep and tangled, reaching down to where the dark things lived. Roots had strength. Roots had permanence. They held you steady when everything else tried to rip you apart. And for the first time, I thought maybe those roots could be real. Maybe they could be enough to grow something that didn't need to be fed by pain or violence.

It wasn't just about being seen. It was about being understood. She made me feel like I was more than the hunger, more than the rage that clawed at my insides. I didn't feel it that night—not the need to purge, not the urge to cleanse. It was still there, coiled deep like a sleeping animal, but it didn't stir. Not when I was with her.

I walked home that night with my hands shoved deep in my pockets, the cold biting at my skin, but I barely felt it. Her smile lingered in my thoughts, softening the edges of everything else. I kept waiting for the craving to creep back in, to scratch at the walls I'd built around it, but it never did. Not that night.

And for the first time, I wondered if this was what it felt like to start over—not in the way the meetings preached, not in the way my grandmother prayed for, but in a way that was mine. Quiet. Subtle. Taking root in places I'd never thought to tend.

Love was a weed. But safety—that required roots. And for once, I didn't mind the idea of planting them.

I walked home that night, my hands shoved in my pockets, her smile still lingering in my thoughts. For the first time, I didn't think about going back to the old ways. The urge was still there, coiled and patient, but it didn't grip me like it used to. I couldn't say why.

Maybe I didn't want to ruin the good things that were starting to grow.

And for the first time in as long as I could remember, I wasn't alone.

THOU SHALT NOT FORGET

Spring, 1995

"…perhaps it is not the act, but the absence of consequences, that truly corrupts the soul."

I stared at the final sentence of my paper. The cursor blinked like a pulse at the end of the line, daring me to second-guess what I'd just written. I didn't. I saved the file, closed the document, and leaned back in the chair that had started to squeak under my weight.

It was a week until graduation.

I had made it—almost. Four years, three months, and ten days clean.

The number sat with me like a whispered confession. It was the same length of time Camille had spoken of the day I first saw her—standing in that folding chair circle, voice soft but unshaken, counting every sober day like a bead on a rosary. I hadn't known then how much weight those words would carry, how they'd echo through my own steps.

Back then, her story felt like a lifeline. Now, it felt like a measuring stick pressed against the raw edge of my soul. I'd caught up to her shadow, and something about that terrified me.

I thought about paging her—just writing the date and tagging it with "143" at the end, our quiet shorthand for love. My thumb hovered over the buttons; the numbers already mapped in my mind. But I couldn't bring myself to do it. The morning felt too hollow, too brittle, like the echo of a prayer left unfinished.

Instead, I set the cordless phone down and looked out the window, watching the world wake up in slow motion. Somewhere out there, Camille was probably doing the same thing—putting on coffee, straightening picture frames, folding yesterday's grief like laundry. And me, I was stuck in the stillness, afraid to move in case something cracked.

Behind me, the sun filtered through the dusty blinds of my grandmother's house, laying stripes across the floor like prison bars. She was still asleep in the next room. I could hear the low hum of her oxygen machine, steady and rhythmic, like a heartbeat that wasn't mine. Most mornings started like this—writing until the world woke up. Breakfast for her. A quick prayer if she was feeling strong. Then work at the library, evening classes, and maybe Camille if I had the energy.

Routine. It kept the cravings at bay.

But the hunger had learned how to wait.

I stood, stretching my back, then walked over to the far corner of the room where the box lived—my scrapbook. Inside: photo album with sealed sheets, black-and-white headlines, glossy color prints of blurred crime scenes, and my own handwritten notes on the margins. The new killer was in there. The Messenger, they were calling him. A clipping from a month prior told a story about a body found near a church parking lot in

North Philly. The words "Hebrews 10:26" had been scrawled in blood across the pavement.

"If we deliberately keep on sinning after we have received the knowledge of the truth, no sacrifice for sins is left…"

I read the verse three times before letting the newspaper drop onto my lap. Something about it was almost… beautiful.

Almost.

I hovered over that article, my fingertip tracing the edge of the ink. "A sermon written in blood… it's always the believers who fall the hardest when they start playing God."

Below that clipping was one from March—Jody LeCornu, shot in her car. Clean kill. No motive. That one bothered me. Too quick. Too cold. Not intimate enough.

"No breath shared. No fear exchanged. A bullet robs the moment of poetry."

Then there was Lisa and Devon Manderach— mother and baby, gone in a moment of twisted desire. The store clerk confessed. It made the papers for weeks. I had followed the story religiously, not because of the brutality—but because of the familiarity. The perpetrator had looked normal. Polite. Hidden in plain sight.

"Evil wears a name tag and rings up your daughter's new shoes."

And beneath that—Terrance Lewis.

Seventeen. West Philly. Wrongfully convicted. No evidence. Just a warm body the system could sacrifice. I circled a sentence in red ink: "Terrance's attorneys argue that he was convicted based on unreliable testimony and withheld evidence."

I wrote just beneath it in neat block letters: THEY'LL NEVER CATCH THE ONES WHO DESERVE IT.

I closed the book, gently, almost reverently. Then I made my way to the kitchen, the hardwood creaking under my feet like it was announcing my every move.

The fridge hummed low as I cracked two eggs into the pan, the sizzle sharp in the quiet. I added salt, a splash of milk—just how she liked it—and stirred slowly, listening for the change in her breathing down the hall.

"Derrick?" Her voice was thin but clear, reaching me from her bedroom.

"Morning, Grandma," I called, flipping the eggs with one hand while grabbing her pill organizer with the other. "Eggs are on. You want toast with it?"

She didn't answer right away. By the time I brought her breakfast on a chipped tray, she was sitting up against her pillows, eyes alert but heavy with the weight of another night.

"You always cook so quiet," she said as I set the tray on her lap. "Nothing like your grandfather. He used to hum gospel when he made my breakfast. You don't hum. You move like you don't want to wake the dead."

I gave her a half-smile. "Well, they've earned their rest."

She chuckled, then coughed, the sound rattling but familiar. I handed her a glass of water.

"You sleep okay?"

"I dreamed your mama was sitting at the edge of my bed. She didn't say nothin'. Just watched me like she was waitin' on something."

I didn't know what to say to that. So I just nodded and adjusted her tray.

"You still writin' them stories?"

"Yeah," I lied. "Still writing."

She looked at me, and for a moment, I wondered if she knew the truth. That I wasn't writing stories anymore. Just collecting them.

"Good," she said, reaching for the fork. "'Cause the Lord gave you a voice. You don't waste what He gave you."

I watched her take the first bite. She closed her eyes as she chewed, like she was trying to remember what joy tasted like.

By the time I slipped out the door, the morning had already fallen into its rhythm—quiet, tired, familiar. I caught the El, then the Sub to campus, my final paper tucked carefully in my bag.

I handed it directly to Professor Halvorsen, seated

behind his desk in that dim little office.

"I'm surprised to see you," he said, flipping through the stapled pages. "You know you didn't need to turn this in, right? Your grades are solid—phenomenal, actually. This assignment was for the ones still scrambling to pass. You're not one of them."

"I know," I said. "But I needed the ritual. The order. The process of finishing something."

He looked up at me over the rim of his glasses, pausing like he was trying to see beyond the surface. Maybe he saw the exhaustion behind my posture, or maybe he just saw a kid holding it together with tape and routine.

"You ever think about writing for real? I mean beyond the classroom?" he asked.

I shrugged. "Sometimes."

"You should. This is excellent work, Derrick. Clear voice. Depth. Control. You've got something most students don't."

"Thanks, Professor. That means a lot."

"You pick up your cap and gown yet?"

"Heading there now."

He nodded and offered a quiet smile. "Well, congratulations. You've earned every bit of it."

I thanked him again and left before the silence stretched too wide between us. Downstairs at the administration office, I signed the clipboard and was handed a thick plastic bag containing my cap, gown, and one of those golden tassels I always thought looked cheap in photos. But when it was mine—when I held it in my hands—it felt heavier than I expected.

I didn't open the bag. Just held it tight against my chest as I stepped out into the thick spring air. The sun was warm, but it didn't reach me. I walked slower than usual, not ready to go home, not ready for what came next.

Everything felt... suspended. Like the city was holding its breath with me.

I ended up wandering through the campus garden, a tucked-away patch of brick paths and wilting azaleas, the kind of place you only found if you weren't looking. I sat on a cold iron bench and stared at the ground, fingers still curled around the plastic handle of the bag.

Graduation was supposed to feel like a finish line. For me, it just felt like a checkpoint in a much darker race.

I should've called Camille. Or paged her. But I didn't.

I remember sitting there, pulling out that day's newspaper from my coat pocket—the one with *The Messenger's* latest kill. The page was worn, edges soft from my thumb tracing the headline. A man found in the basement of a church on 18th Street. Single gunshot wound. Scripture etched into the wall behind him.

James 1:15 — "Then, after desire has conceived, it gives birth to sin; and sin, when it is full-grown, gives birth to death."

The ritual. The message. The mirror.

Whoever this person was, they weren't just killing. They were *communicating*.

And something in me understood the language.

I sat there for a long time, the paper slack in my hands, the scripture echoing through me like a memory I hadn't made yet.

Was it possible to recognize a stranger? To feel the heat of their thoughts before ever seeing their face?

I reached for my journal, tucked into the bottom of my bag, and scribbled this down:

> We are made of sharpened things—
> Blades of guilt, folded with
> discipline. Some carve to forget.
> Others carve to be remembered.
>
> He is not foreign to me. Not truly.
> His marks are clean. His wounds
> speak scripture. And I— I read them
> like confessions.

The page sat heavy in my lap, weighted with more than ink and paper. It was the kind of heaviness that presses against your ribs, reminds you that some truths aren't written—they're carved. Back then, I wouldn't have called it that. Back then, it was just... curiosity. But time has a way of sharpening the edges of things. When you look back, you start to see the lines weren't blurred at all; you just couldn't bring yourself to admit what you were seeing.

I didn't know it then—not really—but the dreams had already started. That's the thing they don't tell you about memories: sometimes, they crawl back into your mind dressed up as nightmares. I used to wake up in a cold sweat, my hands clenched tight, the muscles in my legs stiff and aching like I'd run for miles. I told myself it was just the dreams. But the soreness lingered, threaded itself through my bones and refused to let go.

There's one dream that still clings to me, even after all these years. It always starts the same way—with the cold. That sharp, biting chill that settles deep in your bones, the kind that makes the air feel thin and cruel. I remember the way it needled through the cracks of old windows, slipping in like it had a purpose, curling around my ankles, creeping up my spine. My breath came out in pale plumes, rising and fading into the dark like whispers too fragile to be heard.

I don't remember the place exactly—just shadows and the echo of dripping water, the way sound seemed to flatten against the walls and die there. But I remember how it felt. Like I was standing on the edge of something vast and unyielding. The ground beneath me was hard and uneven, and the air smelled damp and old, like it had been trapped there for decades.

There was a silence, heavy and deliberate, the kind that feels like it's waiting for something. My hands itched with a sensation I couldn't place—a kind of tension, like I'd been gripping something for too long. My fingers would flex and curl, pressing against the empty air, as if testing the weight of it.

And then there were the colors. Red. Bright and sharp, cutting through the darkness like it didn't belong there. The lines stretched across something I couldn't quite make out, deliberate and measured, each stroke clean and intentional. It felt... methodical. Like someone had taken their time with it, made sure every mark was perfect. I remember thinking it wasn't just written—it was inscribed, like the lines themselves held weight.

The dream always ended the same way: with the feeling of something heavy settling into my chest, spreading out like ink in water. It was a slow, creeping sensation—an understanding that never quite reached the surface but lingered just beneath. I would wake up gasping, my hands still clenched, my breath ragged, my heart thrumming with something that felt like fear... or maybe recognition.

And every time I woke, I would lie there staring at the ceiling, feeling the ghost of the cold still clinging to my skin. My hands would throb, knuckles aching, and I'd flex them one by one just to make sure they were still mine.

I never spoke about the dream. Not back then. How could I? I wasn't even sure it was mine to tell.

The night before graduation I woke up sweating. Heart pounding. Hands clenched into fists so tight the tendons burned. I told myself it was just a dream. I told myself that a hundred times. But when I sat up, the ache in my body was real. The soreness in my legs was real.

My shoes were still on.

I remember looking down at them—laces tied, perfectly knotted. But that wasn't the strangest part. It was the plastic.

Clear, heavy-duty plastic, wrapped around the soles in a tight, deliberate fashion. Layers crisscrossed, smooth and taut, like someone had taken their time making sure it wouldn't come loose. I couldn't wrap my head around it. Why would I do that? I bent down, fingers brushing the edges where the plastic had been sealed with duct tape, tight enough that I had to peel it back carefully.

It made no sense. I'd never done that before. My first thought was to blame the dreams—sleepwalking, maybe. I tried to laugh it off, but it didn't sound right. There was no mud, no dirt—just that slick, preserved surface, like I'd gone to great lengths to keep the soles clean. Or to keep something from being left behind.

I yanked the plastic off, bundled it in my hands, and tossed it into the trash. I felt like I should've examined it more, looked closer, but a part of me didn't want to know. I checked the floor for footprints, half expecting to see smears or marks, but it was clean. Too clean. I pressed my hands to my face, rubbed my eyes until the blurriness faded.

I couldn't shake the unease. It gnawed at me, whispering that maybe I wasn't just living vicariously through The Messenger. Maybe I was learning from him. Taking notes. Preparing.

I couldn't admit it then—not even to myself. Back then, I convinced myself it was just curiosity. The way people get caught up in serial killers and murder mysteries, following the patterns, dissecting the motives. That's how I rationalized it. I told myself I was just fascinated. That I was only trying to understand.

But the truth is, I found a certain peace in reading about him. It felt like justice was still out there—harsh and raw, but present. Like someone was balancing the scales when no one else could.

Maybe that's why I clipped every article, studied every line. I wasn't just tracking him. I was respecting him.

Whenever I think about this part of my life a verse always comes to mind. For nothing is hidden that will not be made manifest, nor is anything secret that will not be known and come to light

I didn't know it back then, but the light was already creeping in, cracking through the walls of my memory. I was just too afraid to look.

Graduation morning crept in slow and deliberate, stretching shadows across the walls like they were marking the edges of change. I woke to the kind of stillness that felt heavy, pressing down on my chest, forcing me to breathe slower just to shake it off. I remember the light slipping through the blinds, thin and pale, the way it always did when spring was just starting to crack through winter's grip.

I swung my legs over the edge of the bed, feeling the familiar ache settle into my knees, the tension stretching through my calves. My shoes were still there, neatly placed by the door, laces tied tight. I hesitated before slipping them on, half-expecting to feel the plastic crinkle beneath my feet again. But there was nothing—just leather and grit, the same as always.

The gown hung from the closet door, its dark fabric heavy with expectation. I reached for it, running my hand down the length of it, feeling the weight press back. It didn't feel real. None of it did. Like I was buttoning up someone else's life, straightening their collar, fixing their tie. I remember staring at my reflection, the edges blurred and pale in the mirror's glass, and wondering if I would even recognize myself from the outside.

The cap came next, stiff and awkward. I adjusted it twice, pulling it down over my brow until it settled in place. I almost laughed when I caught my own eyes in the mirror—like I was watching someone else get ready for their own redemption. But I shook off the thought and grabbed the tassel, the thin gold threads coarse under my fingertips. It felt heavier than it looked.

I took a breath, forced my shoulders back, and stepped out into the hallway. The house was quiet, still wrapped in the hush of early morning. I made my way to my grandmother's room, my footsteps soft against the floorboards. I tapped lightly on the door before pushing it open.

She was already dressed—wrapped in her Sunday coat, the one she saved for special occasions, thick wool buttoned up to her chin. Her hands were folded neatly in her lap, fingers curled over one another like she was holding something precious. She smiled when she saw me, her eyes creasing at the edges, and for a moment, the years fell away. She looked like she did when I was young—strong and steady, a pillar rooted deep in faith.

I wheeled her out to the cab, the chill of the morning biting at my cheeks, but I didn't mind. I didn't feel it. Not really. She hummed a hymn as we moved, soft and low, the melody unraveling like a memory she hadn't quite let go of.

We got to the auditorium early—too early, but she insisted. Said she wanted to see everyone arrive, wanted to feel the excitement in the air. I settled her into a good spot near the front easy for Camille to find, made sure she was comfortable before I made my way backstage with the other graduates.

When my name was finally called, I stepped out onto that stage, the lights glaring and hot, applause rolling in like distant thunder. My cap was too tight. The gown too long. Everything about the moment felt borrowed—like I was stepping into someone else's celebration.

But when I looked out and saw my grandmother—wrapped in her Sunday coat, sitting straight in her wheelchair, eyes locked on me like I'd just parted the Red Sea—I felt something in my chest tighten. Not pain. Not pride. Something quieter. It moved through me like peace pretending to be disbelief.

Afterward, Camille helped wheel her outside while I trailed behind, holding my gown.

Grandma took my hand and squeezed it once. "Your mama would've been proud," she said. "Not because you graduated. Because you survived. That's all this life asks of us most days. Not brilliance. Just breath and stubbornness."

Camille stood beside her, smiling, radiant in the glow of everything I couldn't name.

"You hungry?" she asked.

I nodded, but it wasn't food I was hungry for.

Grandma patted Camille's hand. "You two go on ahead. Sister Margie from church is here somewhere—she said she'd take me home."

"You sure?" I asked, already knowing the answer.

"I'm old, baby. Not helpless," she said with a smirk. "Let your girl feed you. Lord knows she probably cooked enough for a family."

Camille laughed, but her eyes flicked to mine, searching. I gave her a small nod.

"Alright," I said, leaning down to kiss Grandma on the cheek. "Call me when you get in."

"I'll be fine. Go enjoy your night. You earned it."

I helped Camille into her car, and as we pulled away, I glanced back and watched Grandma disappear into a small crowd of familiar church faces—smiling, waving, exactly where she belonged.

Camille reached across the console and squeezed my hand, her thumb tracing slow circles against my skin. "You know," she said softly, eyes still on the road, "I've been thinking about tonight for weeks. Staging it in my head like scene from a movie."

I glanced over, the corners of my mouth tugging into something that wasn't quite a smile. "Yeah?"

"Yeah," she said. "You graduating—it's not just a big deal. It's sacred. You did something most people don't come back from. I know what it costs to survive something. The shame. The fear. The nights you want to crawl out of your own skin. I've lived it too. And I wanted tonight to feel like that. a turning point."

Her voice had that calm certainty I remembered from the first time I saw her speak. The way she could wrap truth in silk and make it easier to hold.

"You always talk about rituals," she continued. "Well... I made one for us. Food. Candlelight. Music I know you like. Nothing fancy, just real. Just us."

But somewhere beneath her hope, something else waited—sharp, familiar, and patient.

I looked out the window, heart thudding for reasons I couldn't name. I'd earned this. But what had I become to earn it?

"You think I'll ever stop feeling like I'm faking it?"

She didn't answer right away, just reached over and squeezed my hand again.

"You're not faking it," she said finally. "You're healing. And sometimes that just feels like pretending until it doesn't."

She smiled, satisfied, and turned up the radio just a little. I let the music fill the silence, turned my gaze toward the window, and watched the city blur by.

Streetlights smeared across glass like bleeding stars. Corner boys posted up in shadows. Neon storefronts flickering like they were struggling to stay awake. The world didn't know I'd made it. Didn't care. And neither did the part of me that still twitched under my skin.

The part that remembered blood.

I thought about The Messenger again—his scripture, his stillness. The way his kills didn't scream. They whispered. A different kind of hunger. Calculated. Holy, even. It should've disgusted me. Instead, it hummed in my chest like a second heart.

Was he out there now? Planning another verse? Another name to cross off some private list of sins?

Or was I just seeing myself in his shadow— reaching for that old feeling, that cold euphoria, like someone brushing a scar just to remember where it hurt.

We pulled into her apartment complex just after dusk. The porch light was already on, casting a soft golden haze across the steps. Camille unlocked the door and led me inside, the scent of rosemary and garlic thick in the air.

"I made your favorite," she said, slipping her shoes off at the door. "Well, one of them. The others were above my pay grade."

The lights were low. A single candle flickered on the kitchen table, next to a scratched-up CD player humming something slow and smoky. The table was set, but the food wasn't out yet.

Camille walked straight to the oven, cracking it open to release a soft wave of heat and the rich scent of something well-seasoned and cornbread. She slipped on a pair of mitts and pulled out two covered dishes, steam fogging the air as she moved with quiet confidence.

"Go get cleaned up," she said over her shoulder, setting the hot trays gently on the counter. "It'll only take me a second to plate everything."

I hesitated, eyes lingering on the way she moved—so calm, so sure. Like she really believed tonight could fix something.

"You sure?"

She looked back at me and smiled. "Go. You'll feel better."

I nodded and disappeared down the hall toward the bathroom, the sound of drawers opening, and plates being set behind me like background music to a moment I wasn't sure I belonged in. For a moment, we just looked at each other.

"You okay?" she asked.

I nodded. Lied.

"Just tired. Long day."

She smiled softly, not buying it but not pushing either. "Well, let's eat before it gets cold."

And we did. At least with our hands.

Camille talked while we ate—soft and steady, her voice rising and falling like a warm breeze across cracked pavement. Her eyes lit up with every memory she tried to stitch into the moment, every hope she dared to put into words.

She gestured gently between bites, punctuating her thoughts with quick glances toward me, searching for something—connection, maybe. Or reassurance.

She leaned in at one point, elbows on the table,

her expression wide with tenderness and anticipation, like this night was the first brick in a new life she believed we could build together.

I nodded in all the right places, chewed when I should've spoken, smiled when her voice broke a little from emotion.

She thirsted for connection. I was just trying not to drown in my own thoughts.

"So what's next for you?" she finally asked, her voice low but direct. "Now that school's done. Are you going to apply to that MFA program you mentioned?"

I swallowed before answering. "Maybe. I haven't really thought it through."

"You should," she said, almost instantly. "You've got a gift, Derrick. Don't let it sit in a drawer collecting dust."

I nodded, unsure how to tell her that my mind wasn't in any drawer—it was locked in a room with no windows.

She tried again. "You gonna keep working at the library? Or is that just for now?"

"Just for now," I said. "Figuring things out."

She gave a small smile and leaned forward, resting her chin on her hand. "I used to think graduating meant everything got clearer. But really, it just gives you better questions."

I looked at her then, really looked—how badly she wanted to believe this was a beginning.

"Yeah," I said quietly. "I guess we'll see."

She smiled and stood, brushing a crumb from her lap. "Powder room. Don't disappear on me."

I watched her walk down the hall, her silhouette soft in the candlelight. When the door clicked shut, I let my gaze drift across the table.

That's when I saw it.

The knife.

It was sitting halfway inside the cornbread pan, its silver edge slick with melted butter. Not placed there with care—just resting. Like it had been used, forgotten, left to cool.

I stood without thinking, the chair barely making a sound against the floor. Walked around the table. Stared at it.

It was beautiful in a way only dangerous things can be. The handle, black and smooth. The blade, sharp and unapologetic.

I reached for it.

Held it.

Admired the way the candlelight danced along the edge.

A thought whispered through me: *If I killed Camille tonight... would I be the first suspect?*

Of course I would. The boyfriend. The last one seen. The one with the storybook ending.

But then again... maybe not. Maybe I'd be the grieving man with a diploma in one hand and a burial suit in the other.

My pulse hammered in my jaw. The knife felt like it belonged there, in my hand, like something I'd misplaced years ago and finally found again.

Then I heard the soft creak of the bathroom door opening.

Camille stepped out slowly, something small and pale clutched in her hand. Her eyes met mine across the flickering glow of the room—first soft, then sharp.

She saw the knife.

Her smile faded.

Her eyes dropped to my hands, then darted back to my face.

I didn't move at first. Then I did.

One step.

Toward her.

She took a slight step back, almost imperceptible, like her body responded before her mind could catch up.

The air between us thinned. Candlelight threw shadows like the room was holding its breath.

I moved toward her—slow, but with intent. Each step measured like it mattered, like I was testing gravity itself. The knife hung at my side, not raised, not hidden. Just... present.

Camille's body shifted. Her arm bent slightly as she tucked whatever was in her hand closer to her chest. She didn't speak. Didn't ask. But her foot slid back again, quiet and cautious, like she was deciding whether to run or believe in me.

My mind buzzed with static. Not rage. Not even impulse. Just a pulse-deep curiosity:

What would happen if I crossed the last inch?

I hadn't realized how tightly I was gripping it until that moment. Her eyes looked to the blade, then back to me, and it was like I'd been dragged from somewhere far away. The weight of it pulled at my wrist, the cold steel whispering its comfort.

Her breath caught—just once, barely audible. And that sound, that fragile little thing, split something open in me.

Then she smiled.

Not wide. Not easy. But real—like someone offering a hand in the dark.

She held out what was in her palm—delicate, trembling. Her voice barely rose above the hum of the room, but it carried the weight of something eternal.

"There's something growing inside me too," she said, like she was reciting a secret she hadn't dared to write down until now.

My eyes dropped to the test—pink lines clear as confession.

"We're expecting," she whispered, her voice a thread of light across the room.

I forced my fingers to loosen, one by one. I didn't look her in the eye. I couldn't. And just like that, the knife in my hand felt less like a key and more like a curse.

I didn't speak right away. Couldn't.

The room was silent except for the candle's soft hiss and the distant hum of the refrigerator, both sounds somehow too loud in that moment.

Inside, something cracked.

I looked at her—the life forming behind her ribs—and felt something ancient and violent rise in my throat. Not hatred. Not fear. Just...

pressure. The kind that builds behind a dam right before it breaks.

What does a killer do when the world dares to bloom in front of him?

I had prepared myself to spill blood. Not build a legacy.

But there she stood, holding both—future and forgiveness—in a trembling hand.

The knife felt foreign now, too heavy to lift, too sharp to justify. It wasn't just a blade anymore. It was a mirror.

And in it, I saw the thing I almost became.

I set the knife down on the table, slow and deliberate, like it might shatter if I moved too fast. The sound it made—barely a clink—felt louder than a gunshot.

She didn't flinch.

I crossed the rest of the space between us, reached out, and pulled her in.

Her body was warm. Real. A pulse against my chest that didn't belong to me. I held her tighter than I should have, and she let me. Her hand, still holding the test, pressed lightly against my back.

There were no words. Just breath—just the quiet surrender of something breaking open and something else holding it together.

Later that night, I walked home alone. Camille offered to drive me, but I told her I needed the air. Truth was, I needed the silence. The kind only a long walk through a sleeping neighborhood can give you.

When I reached the house, the porch light was still on. Grandma was already in bed. I should've gone inside. Should've gone straight to my room.

But something tugged at me.

I circled around the back, toward the old shed near the fence line. The trash cans were still out by the curb, so I went to pull them in. A simple task. Mindless. Familiar.

That's when I noticed the dirt.

Just a little off. Like it had been turned recently. Stirred, then smoothed over. I stepped closer. A few low branches brushed my arm as I moved past them. And there—half-buried beneath the shrubs, hidden like a memory that didn't want to be found—was the box.

The old one. The one I hadn't touched in years.

I didn't even need to open it to know what was inside. The weight of it alone told the story. My fingers hovered over the latch, hesitation clawing its way up my spine.

For a long moment, I just stood there. My hand rested on the lid, feeling the cool metal beneath my palm. It felt alive. Like it was waiting for me to come back. I sucked in a breath, let it out slow, and flipped the latch.

The lid creaked as it opened, hinges whining like they'd been frozen in place. Inside, the air was stale—trapped and undisturbed. I pulled back the flaps of old cloth, fingers brushing against the hard surface of something wrapped tightly in plastic.

I peeled it back, layer by layer, revealing the face of an old, leather-bound journal. Its edges were frayed, worn from handling. I knew it before I even touched it. The weight of it was familiar, like holding a confession bound in skin.

The leather was cracked along the spine, the surface worn smooth from fingers tracing its surface. I flipped it open, and my breath stilled in my chest.

The first page was blank, but I could see the indentations of handwriting—faint, like it had been pressed hard enough to bleed through. I ran my fingers over the marks, feeling the grooves of the letters. I turned the page, and that's when I saw it.

Genesis 4:10 — "The voice of your brother's blood cries out to me from the ground."

The scripture was written in red ink, neat and precise, the letters pressed into the page with deliberate care. Beneath it, a name. *Katherine Wills. December 4th, 1992.* And just below that, a single, perfect fingerprint. Dark and smeared, like whoever wrote the verse had sealed it with their own mark.

I turned the page again.

Exodus 20:13 — "Thou shalt not kill."
Richard Harlow. March 8th, 1993.

The same bloody fingerprint marked its place, pressed neatly beneath the name like a signature.

I kept turning, my heart pounding harder with each page. The names were lined up neatly, one after another, each one chronicled with its own verse. Scripture I recognized. Verses that spoke of blood, of retribution, of judgment.

Each entry was written with almost reverent care. Names, dates, scripture—and always that print. A small testament left behind, as if the writer were sealing the page with their own absolution.

The further I flipped, the more the verses bled into one another. The ink grew darker, the lines deeper. My fingers grazed one of the entries and came back smudged with something dark, something that clung to my skin like oil.

I stared at my hand, heart thudding in my ears. My thumb brushed the edge of the page, smearing the ink. I rubbed my fingers together, watching the faint stain spread across my fingertips. It didn't smell like ink. It didn't flake like ink.

I flipped back to the beginning, studying each fingerprint. They were all different. Some partial, some whole, like the mark was made hastily, pressed too fast. But each one was deliberate. Each one stained with that same dark, unyielding crimson.

I flipped to the last page, my breath catching in my throat. The scripture number was scrawled across the top in jagged strokes:

Luke 8:17 — "For nothing is hidden that will not be made manifest, nor is anything secret that will not be known and come to light."

And there, beneath the verse, was the fingerprint. It was darker than the rest, pressed deeper into the page like it had been branded there. A shrine to secrecy. A promise in red.

I stared at it. Time froze, stretched out in brittle lines around me. My fingers hovered over the letters, trembling. I blinked, once, twice, as if the words would rearrange themselves if I just looked hard enough. But they didn't. They stayed the same. Permanent. Inked into the ledger like a covenant.

I closed the book, my breath rattling out of me in a rush. My hands were shaking, my legs unsteady as I shoved the journal back into the box, clapping the lid shut before I could change my mind.

For a long time, I just stood there, my hand still on the box, knuckles white against the metal latch. The shadows stretched long around me, pooling at my feet, clinging to my shoes.

I knew what I had seen. I just wasn't ready to admit it.

The light was already creeping in, cracking through the walls of my memory. I was just too afraid to look.

And then it hit me—like a match dragged across old bone—painful, familiar, flaring:

The church basement. The scripture. The sharpness of the act. The way the light had looked on blood.

Not from the paper.

From behind the eyes.

And just like that, it wasn't memory. It wasn't curiosity.

It was recognition.

The scripture had always sounded too familiar. The angles, the wounds, the ritual of it all—too precise, too known.

Not read. Recalled.

I stood there with my hand still on the latch, and for the first time, the silence didn't feel empty.

It felt ritualistic—like something had been waiting for me to come home.

In that moment, I realized something that didn't just empty me—it echoed through every quiet place I thought I'd healed.

My sobriety had only lived in my mind. My body had been moving, working, remembering without me.

Whatever peace I thought I'd earned was nothing more than a lie told in the language of forgetting. And the body never forgets.

THOU SHALT GUARD THE INNOCENT

One year later

A year had passed, and everything looked different—but not everything had changed.

The church was full of faces wrapped in black. Camille stood beside me, our infant daughter asleep against her chest in a white bonnet far too bright for the room. I held her hand, though neither of us said a word.

My grandmother had passed like a hymn fading into silence—not vanished, but released, like the final breath of a prayer too tired to hold on.

The prayers had outlived the body. The hands that raised me now rested beneath linen and lilies. She wasn't just dead— she had been called home in a voice older than time.

She died the way she lived—praying. Peacefully, in her sleep, gospel playing on low in the background. It was Camille who found her. I couldn't. I had just put the baby down.

Now we stood here in front of her casket, dressed in the kind of clothes people wear to say goodbye. The preacher's voice droned on behind us, quoting scripture about time and eternity. Something about seeds and harvest.

The choir sang one of her favorites—"His Eye is on the Sparrow"—but no voice rose quite like Sister May's in the second row, her notes cracking like the sky might open. I remember how my grandmother used to hum that song while folding sheets or brushing the edge of my collar on Sunday mornings. She said it was a reminder that even the smallest life could still be held by grace. That God's hands were big enough to cradle the broken. I didn't understand it then. But standing in that church, with my daughter pressed against Camille's chest and the scent of lilies curling around my grief, I did.

I looked over, and she nodded—an unspoken invitation. I reached out, carefully, gently sliding my hands beneath our daughter, lifting her from Camille's arms. She settled into me like she knew it was safe, her cheek pressed against my shoulder, tiny fingers curling into my shirt. Camille stepped closer, resting her head against my other shoulder. I stood there, holding them both, feeling the weight of their breath, the trust in their touch.

My grandmother used to tell me that love was measured by what you could hold. I didn't understand it back then—thought she was just talking about carrying groceries or lifting boxes at church events. But standing there with my daughter in one arm and Camille leaning into me with her grief, I understood. Love was weight. And I was learning how to carry it.

The preacher's voice finally fell quiet, and the silence that followed felt sacred. I leaned over and kissed Camille's temple.

"She would've been proud of you," she whispered.
I didn't answer. Just nodded, blinking against the sting behind my eyes.

I was focused on the way Camille's hand kept tightening around mine every few minutes, grounding me. Or maybe testing me—to see if I was still here.

I was.

One year sober.

For real this time.

Not just in my mind, but in my bones. In the ache behind my eyes when I didn't take my prescribed sleep aids. In the way my hands stayed empty at night. In the way my daughter's breath against my neck made me feel clean.

Diary Entry — April 15, 1996

I didn't say anything. Not when
the preacher asked if anyone
wanted to speak. Not when the
choir sang the first note of "His Eye
is on the Sparrow." I just held my
daughter a little closer, felt her
breath against my chest, and kept
my mouth shut.

But I wanted to. I wanted to say a thousand things. I wanted to tell them how she would pray so hard some mornings her knees would creak, how she believed the power of God could fit inside a single breath if you just knew how to ask. I wanted to tell them how she sang off-key while she cooked, humming the same hymn she hummed while she folded my clothes when I was still small enough to think monsters only lived under the bed.

I wanted to tell them how she saved me. How she wrapped her hands around mine when I came back from the streets, blood still fresh under my nails. How she didn't ask questions—just whispered a prayer and told me to wash up. How she cooked for me, even when I hadn't earned it. How she prayed for me louder than I ever screamed.

But the words stayed stuck in my throat, tangled with memories I still haven't forgiven myself for. So I just stood there, my daughter cradled in my arms, and watched them bury the only person who ever saw the good in me when I couldn't see it myself.

And now, I've got her. This tiny thing that looks at me like I'm worthy. Like I'm not the sum of all the things I've buried. She's just learning how to smile, how to reach out and hold my finger like it's the only thing keeping her steady. I don't know how to be a father. I don't know how to be half of what my grandmother saw in me. But when I hold her... it feels possible. Like maybe the prayers didn't fall on deaf ears. Like maybe the monsters under the bed can't reach this far.

I almost said all of that at the funeral. But I didn't. Because sometimes words aren't meant to be spoken — they're meant to be held. Kept close. Guarded like something fragile.

> I'll try to make you proud,
> Grandma. I swear I will.

I closed the journal and ran my fingers over the worn leather cover, the edges fraying where my hands had gripped it too tight over the years. Writing had always been easier than speaking — my thoughts flowed better when there was no one to interrupt, no eyes watching for cracks in the facade. I could bleed onto the page, hide the mess in metaphors, and walk away feeling lighter.

That night after the funeral, I sat by the window with the bottle of pills on the sill, watching the way the streetlights stretched shadows across the pavement. The world outside moved as if nothing had changed, but inside, something had shifted.

I took the pills now, yes. Doctor-approved. Small and white and lined up like soldiers in my drawer. But they kept the shadows out. Kept the old dreams where they belonged — in the past. At least most nights. The sleep was dreamless, thick and heavy, like sinking into a body of water where no light could reach. I used to wake up drenched in sweat, fists clenched around ghosts I couldn't shake. But now, I woke up still. Calm. Blank.

Sometimes I wondered if it was the pills themselves that killed the dreams, or if it was just me—finally letting go of what I had held onto for too long. Camille would watch me sometimes, her eyes soft but searching, like she wanted to ask if they were working. If the ghosts still found their way in. I'd nod, offer a small smile, and she'd accept it—grateful for the lie, or maybe just choosing to believe it.

The truth was, I couldn't remember the last time I dreamed. And maybe that was a blessing. My nights were clean now—empty of memory, untouched by the sharp edges of what I'd done. I slept through storms, through silence, through the soft cries of my daughter in the next room. Camille would bring her to me in the morning, her eyes bright and curious, and I'd hold her close, burying my face in her warmth, the smell of innocence clinging to her skin.

There were mornings I would sit at the kitchen table, the sunlight stretching across the hardwood, and feel... almost normal. I'd sip my coffee, listen to Camille hum softly as she made breakfast, and I'd believe—if only for a moment— that the darkness had finally given up its hold.

But I knew better. The silence wasn't surrender. It was just waiting.

Camille said I smiled more. That I laughed in my sleep. That sometimes I even talked to God again. She'd say it offhandedly, while folding clothes or stirring a pot on the stove, her eyes glancing up just enough to catch my reaction. I never knew how to respond, so I'd just nod and let the silence do the talking. But sometimes, late at night when the house settled into its quiet rhythm, I'd wonder if it was true.

Maybe I did smile more. Maybe the laughter wasn't just muscle memory anymore. Maybe the ache that lived in my bones had loosened its grip, just enough for something lighter to slip in. And as for God...well, maybe I did speak to Him. Not in the way I used to—not with desperation or demands. More like a whisper beneath my breath, a silent acknowledgment that I was still here. That I was still trying.

My job was quiet, respectable. I helped shape the words of others—academic journals, college newsletters, the occasional speech for someone who liked to sound smarter than they were. It wasn't glamorous, but it was honest. It gave me structure—something to hold onto when the past threatened to unravel me. I would sit at my desk, red pen in hand, correcting the sentences of men who had never walked the streets I had, who had never folded their hands in prayer over blood that wouldn't come off. I fixed their words, made them sharper, clearer, more refined. Sometimes, I wished I could do the same with memory.

But it was fatherhood that truly anchored me. A redemption I hadn't asked for but showed up anyway—an unearned grace wrapped in blankets and soft cries at midnight. My daughter looked at me like I was the whole sky. Like I held up the stars just for her. Every diaper change felt like a prayer. Every time I rocked her back to sleep, I felt like I was mending something in myself I couldn't name. She had this way of resting her hand on my chest while I held her, her fingers stretching and curling like she was feeling for my heartbeat, making sure it was still there.

I'd sit with her in the rocking chair, the rhythm of it pulling us both into something close to peace. I would watch her eyelids grow heavy, her tiny hands still clutching at my shirt like she was afraid I'd let go. I never did. I wouldn't. Sometimes I'd whisper promises to her in the dark, things I'd never say in the light of day. I told her she'd never have to know the things I knew. That I'd hold back the darkness, that I'd guard her from it, even if it killed me.

And as I rocked her, the weight of her pressed to my chest, I felt something break and rebuild inside me, over and over again. Like her heartbeat was stitching me back together, one breath at a time.

Camille would sometimes peek in from the doorway, her smile soft and sad, like she was watching a miracle she never thought she'd see. She never interrupted. She just let me have that space, that time with my daughter, like she knew it was sacred. Like she knew I was learning how to be a father one heartbeat at a time.

Fatherhood wasn't just a blessing. It was a reckoning. A chance to hold innocence in my hands and swear to whatever God still listened that it wouldn't be lost on my watch. Not this time.

I still reflect on the nights I would stand in the doorway of my daughter's room, watching her sleep. Her tiny breaths rising and falling with the kind of peace I had long since forgotten. I'd rest my hand on the frame, fingers brushing the wood like I was searching for splinters, something to ground me to the moment. In those quiet hours, I would think about the man I used to be—the weight of him, the shadow he cast. How easy it would be for him to seep back in, to crawl out of whatever corner I had forced him into. But the softness of her breathing, the way her hand would curl around the edge of her blanket, kept him at bay. She was my tether. My proof that redemption wasn't just something you whispered in church; it was something you held onto for dear life.

I sleep now, but I keep the door locked. Not out of fear. But out of reverence for what still lingers beneath my skin.

But out of respect for what still knocks.

Lord, if You still hear me— thank You for lending me this moment, for letting me stand in the warmth of her memory, and not the cold shadow of who I used to be.

Thank You for steady hands, even when they tremble. For the sleep that comes with effort, and the dreams that no longer draw blood.

And for this child, this tiny thing with lungs strong enough to pull me back into the world each morning. She cries like her voice matters, and I listen like it might save me.

Watching her grow is like watching time repent. Each coo, each step, each stubborn scream—it teaches me how to stay human. How to stay here.

The urges haven't left entirely. They hover. Wait. Whisper. But the pills help—lined up in rows like quiet guards. The door stays locked at night, not out of fear, but to remind myself that control is something I choose now.

And The Messenger?

There hasn't been a mention of him in months. Not in the papers. Not in the whispers. I thought the silence would bring peace, but it only made me listen harder—to the shadows, to the stillness, to myself. But I don't need the headlines to remember what I buried.

He wasn't a myth or a monster lurking in the dark. He was a version of me, spoken in blood and verses, built in silence, and sharpened through ache.

He was the scripture. I was the silence. And I am what survived them both.

I live differently now.

My days are built on schedules—feedings, deadlines, walks through the park where I carry her small body against my chest like armor. Her weight is the only kind that grounds me.

Work is steady. Editing reports, shaping language for people who rarely mean what they say. I sharpen their words, make them sound better, clearer. It's easier to fix other people's sentences than my own past.

Camille says I'm becoming the man I once pretended to be. I don't argue. Not because I agree, but because I want to.

And in those quiet moments—changing diapers in the dark, humming lullabies I didn't know I knew—I start to believe her.

I show up. Every day.

That's all my grandmother ever asked of me.

To show up. To guard the innocent.

Even now, I hear her voice in the smallest things—how I fold my daughter's clothes, how I say grace before dinner, how I step into each day like it owes me nothing and still give thanks for its breath.

> "Fear not, for I have redeemed you;
>
> I have called you by name, you are Mine.
>
> When you pass through the waters, I will be with you;
>
> and through the rivers, they shall not overwhelm you.
>
> When you walk through fire you shall not be burned,
>
> and the flame shall not consume you." - Isaiah 43:1–2a

I read that one night when the house was quiet, and the bottle of pills felt heavier than usual.

And for the first time in a long time, I believed it wasn't just written for saints and survivors.

It was written for people like me—people who came through the fire and still carried the smell of smoke in their clothes.

Most nights, the house sleeps before I do.

I sit in the hallway sometimes, between her nursery and our bedroom, just listening. The sound of her soft breathing. Camille's quiet turning in bed. The hum of the fridge, the creak in the floorboard by the stairs—it all reminds me I'm still here.

Alive.
Needed.
Present.

There are moments I catch myself studying the lock on the front door, wondering if it's strong enough. Not because I expect anyone to break in—but because I know what it means to live with something that could wake up at any moment, clawing to get out.

I read once that sleepwalkers can cook, drive, even eat—without knowing. The body, they say, can rehearse routines long after the mind has left the room.

That's what it felt like.

Not rage. Not impulse. Just motion without meaning—ritual without awareness. I wasn't absent. I was elsewhere.

Some part of me knew exactly what to do. The rest of me just didn't show up to stop it.

I became The Messenger—moving with purpose, but without presence.

My body had memory, even when my mind was in exile.

And when I finally woke up, I didn't recognize the footprints I'd left behind—
just blood where my conscience should've been.

Everyone thinks I've been clean over five years now.

I let them think that. I never corrected the math.

But the truth is, I've only truly been clean for one.

That night in Camille's kitchen was my real Day One.

The rest of it—the speeches, the chips, the meetings—I was chasing the idea of sobriety while my body stayed haunted.

So no, I don't wear the chip on my keyring anymore.

Because this time, I'm not collecting milestones.

I'm just trying to live like I deserve the air I breathe.

Camille and I were sitting on the couch one night, the kind of night when silence doesn't feel heavy, just shared. The TV was off. The baby monitor glowed softly on the end table.

She looked over at me, legs tucked beneath her, eyes warm and patient. "You've been quiet lately."

"I think I'm still catching up to myself," I said.

She nodded slowly. "Sometimes I watch you from across the room and wonder what you're holding onto. What you're still afraid of."

"You ever feel like you're trying to live like the man people think you already are?"

She didn't flinch. "Yeah. All the time."

I let out a breath I hadn't realized I was holding. "It's just… some days, I feel like I've got it all under control. And others—it's like I'm just waiting for the part of me I can't trust to wake up."

She moved closer, rested her head against my shoulder. "You know what I see? A man who didn't walk away. A man who didn't disappear."

"I didn't tell you everything," I said after a pause. "About the early days. About when the sobriety was only in my head."

She didn't move, didn't ask for more. Just let the silence speak.

"It wasn't real until that night," I added. "You. The kn... The test. That was the moment everything snapped into place."

She pulled back enough to look me in the eye. "You don't owe me the clean version. Just the honest one."

Before I could respond, the baby monitor crackled, and our daughter's cries filled the room.

I stood up. "I got her."

She watched me as I walked down the hallway, and for the first time in a long time, I felt worthy of being seen. Once I got my daughter settled down, I didn't return to the conversation. I look back on that day and I wonder now if it was intentional, like it was too soon for a confession… Perhaps I just wanted to be alone.

The house was wrapped in a hush that felt almost reverent. I lingered in the doorway of her room, watching her chest rise and fall, her tiny fingers curled into fists that would someday reach for more than just my hand. For a moment, I stayed like that, my hand pressed against the doorframe, feeling the weight of it. The heaviness of knowing that whatever darkness I carried, it could never reach her—not while I was still breathing.

Camille called softly from the hallway, her voice pulling me back. I kissed my daughter's forehead, her skin warm and soft, and pulled the door until it clicked shut, sealing her inside that bubble of innocence I swore to protect.

The hallway stretched long and quiet before me, the shadows pooling at the edges like they were waiting for me to come closer. I moved slowly, feeling the ache in my bones that never quite went away, the reminders of who I used to be.

My hand slipped into my pocket, fingers curling around the familiar weight of the pill bottle. I didn't think twice.

I unscrewed the cap, the soft rattle of tablets against plastic punctuating the silence. I shook one into my hand, small and white, chalky against my palm. Doctor-approved. Safe. That's what they said, anyway. But I knew better. They weren't just for sleep. They were for silence. For muting the whispers that sometimes crept up on me in the quiet. For stilling the echoes of things I could never quite forget.

I popped the pill, dry-swallowed it, and leaned back against the hallway wall, letting the cool plaster seep into my spine. I closed my eyes and waited for it to do its job. To flatten out the memories. To quiet the questions. To dull the edge of everything I'd sharpened over the years.

When I opened my eyes, the world had settled into something softer, more manageable. The whispers faded back into the shadows, and the silence became bearable again. I pushed off the wall, made my way to our bedroom, and slid under the covers beside Camille. Her breathing was steady, the kind of rhythm you only get when sleep isn't something you have to fight for.

I stared at the ceiling for a long time, waiting for the pill to work its final magic. My eyelids grew heavy, the shadows in the corners of the room softened and blurred. I closed my eyes and drifted—no dreams, no whispers, just the soft blackness I'd learned to crave.

The Next Morning – At the Office

The sun spilled through the blinds of my office, pooling across the desk in wide streaks of light. I sat with my coffee cup steaming beside me, the surface still rippling from the first pour. My hands were steady, the kind of steady that comes with routine, with knowing exactly what the next hour would bring.

I took a slow sip, the heat tracing its way down my throat, pooling in my stomach like fire. The radio on the corner shelf hummed with low chatter—weather, traffic, the same mundane noise that acted as my morning backdrop. It lulled me into that familiar space, where the world was predictable, manageable.

I tapped my pen against the desk, listening to the muffled hum of phones ringing beyond my office door. My inbox was stacked with documents— revisions on policy briefs, notes from the higher-ups on language that needed to be more "palatable." I was halfway through editing a paragraph on sustainable development when the static on the radio cracked, sharp and insistent.

"BREAKING: MURDER IN FRANKFORD— CROSS FOUND AT SCENE."

My hand hovered over the keyboard, fingers still poised mid-stroke. The coffee cup settled onto the desk with a soft clink, steam curling up and dissipating in the morning light.

My heart didn't race. My hands didn't shake.

But something ancient in me blinked once. And kept watching.

"Police say a wooden cross, possibly left by the assailant, was recovered from the scene. DNA was found on it—sweat, maybe blood. They're running it through national databases. There's also mention of a witness. Someone who caught a glimpse of the suspect fleeing the area."

The words dripped into the room like rainwater from a cracked ceiling, slow and insidious. I leaned back in my chair, fingers interlacing behind my head as I stared at the radio, its red light blinking in sync with the words.

"Authorities are investigating whether this might be connected to a string of unsolved murders believed to be the work of a serial killer known as 'The Messenger.' With a possible DNA match and a witness description, officials believe the city may soon have answers—and closure."

The lines of my coffee cup blurred, the edges softening like they were melting into the desk. I swallowed hard, my throat dry. Outside, the world moved along at its regular pace, cars honking, people walking—oblivious to the shadows that stretched just a little longer that morning.

I tried to focus, turning back to my screen, but the words wouldn't settle. They hovered just behind my eyes, flickering like the afterimage of a camera flash. My hands moved on autopilot, typing out corrections and adjusting margins, but I couldn't shake the feeling that something had been set loose. Something that had been waiting in the dark, patient and quiet, just watching.

I stood up, crossed the room to the window, and stared out at the city below. People moved like clockwork, crossing streets, huddling under umbrellas as the rain started to fall. My reflection stared back at me, pale and unblinking, the dark circles under my eyes more pronounced in the morning light.

I exhaled, a slow measured breath, and watched it fog up the glass. My mind traced the words from the radio, one by one, replaying them like a song you can't forget. The cross. The witness. The DNA.

I ran my fingers along the windowsill, feeling the dust collect under my fingertips. I'd cleaned it just last week, but the city had a way of leaving its mark.

I reached for my phone, the motion deliberate, almost forced. My thumb hovered over Camille's number before I pulled back. What would I even say? What words could I choose that didn't feel like I was tipping off fate?

I turned back to my desk, but the air felt different now—thicker, like I was wading through it. The broadcaster's voice still crackled from the radio, looping through the same details, each pass pressing them deeper into my skull.

The suspect is described as a white male, balding, between five-seven and five-eleven, estimated around two hundred pounds," the anchor added. *"Police are working with a composite sketch based on the eyewitness account."*

I leaned back in my chair, fingers still tapping on the desk, eyes fixed on the radio, waiting for the crackle to settle back into static. My breath came out slow, controlled, a habit I had learned over time to mask the storms inside.

A white male.
Balding.
Five-seven to five-eleven.

I almost laughed, the sound escaping more like a scoff than anything else. I ran my hands over my own hair, thick and unruly, my skin a shade that had never seen pale. For a moment, the tension that had coiled itself around my spine like barbed wire began to loosen. I sat up, straightening my posture, the weight slipping from my shoulders like dust shaken off after a long walk.

Outside, the city moved on, unaware of my brief unraveling. The rain had started to fall in earnest now, tapping softly against the glass, a rhythm that seemed to ground me back into place. I watched the droplets race each other down the windowpane, their paths crossing and splitting, finding their way home.

I stood up and walked back to the window, leaning against the sill and looking out over the city as the broadcaster moved on to local sports updates and weather. My reflection stared back at me, brown eyes framed by shadows, and I let out a breath I hadn't realized I'd been holding.

I knew better than to let my guard down entirely, but in that moment, there was a flash of something—relief, maybe. Like the universe had thrown me a lifeline, if only for a moment. I reached for my coffee cup, the ceramic warm and familiar in my hands, and took a slow sip, savoring the bitterness that grounded me back to reality.

I didn't need to be told twice; I knew how the world saw me. Knew how it measured me, weighed me. I'd spent years navigating its assumptions, sidestepping its judgments. But this? This was different. I wasn't on the menu this time.

Not today.

The radio continued its steady hum of trivialities—school closures, city council meetings, a new bakery opening on 6th and Main. I let it fade into the background, a lullaby of normalcy as I sat back down at my desk and reached for my pen.

And for a moment, just a moment, I allowed myself to breathe.

I turned back to my screen, the hum of the office returning like a tide. Reports waited. Deadlines loomed. And somewhere behind the glass walls and fluorescent light, the world kept pretending it made sense.

The phone rang twice that morning—one call from a client needing edits on a keynote address, another from a professor who liked the sound of his own metaphors more than the structure holding them together. I made notes, flagged a few lines for rewrite, and filed the requests into digital folders named for people who probably wouldn't remember my name.

It was quiet work. Careful work. The kind that demanded attention but rarely praise.

But it gave me something I needed: routine.

By noon, the noise outside my window had thinned to birds and passing traffic. I leaned back, stretched, and glanced at the photo on my desk— Camille holding our daughter in the garden, her little hands reaching up like she wanted to pull the sky down.

That was the only reminder I needed.

Later that evening, I was home. The house smelled like lavender and warm milk. Camille was folding laundry on the couch, and the baby was babbling in her playpen, a plastic giraffe hanging by its neck from her fist.

She saw me and grinned, her gums pink and shiny.

I walked over and scooped her up, spinning her gently until she squealed.

"Daddy's home," I said into her neck, breathing in her innocence like it could cleanse something old in me.

Camille smiled without looking up. "Bath time's yours tonight."

"Gladly."

I took our daughter down the hall, her tiny fingers tugging at the collar of my shirt. The door clicked shut behind us.

And for a little while, the world felt exactly as it should.

But as I lowered her into the warm water, the air shifted— a hush like memory, a tremble in the walls. The kind of stillness that wraps around you, not to comfort, but to remind you that something sacred is watching.

In the corner of the room, something flickered. Not shadow. Not light.

Just presence— a quiet manifestation of something long buried.

And there he was: not a ghost, not a hallucination, but a boy made of breath and ache, the shape of everything I lost when the world stopped being kind.

His skin was smudged with childhood. My breath caught—not from fear, but from recognition. A part of me remembered what it was like to be that small, that weightless, that untouched by ruin.. His eyes wide with questions I never got to ask.

He looked like he had just stepped out of a memory still soft with wonder, still unscarred by what would come.

He didn't speak—he didn't have to. His gaze fell on my daughter, then returned to me, as if to ask: Did you make it out for both of us?

I wanted to say yes. Wanted to say more. But all I could do was reach for the washcloth, run it slow across her back, and whisper the only vow I could give:

"You'll never meet the world that found me too early."

"You'll never know the sharp edge of silence before you've learned how to speak. You'll never carry the weight of grown-up pain in a child's bones. You'll never be handed a world made of broken glass and told to build a home from it.

As long as I breathe, the darkness will stop at this door. The ache will end with me. And every day I wake up, I'll be the wall between you and the war I was born into."

When I looked again, the corner was empty. But something in me stayed kneeling before the presence, tending to water and memory, like I was baptizing the air to keep the past from breathing too loud.

She splashed once, smiling like she already knew she was safe.

And I believed her.

THOU SHALT RETURN WITH PURPOSE

September 2015

Luke 11:24–26 — *"When an unclean spirit goes out of a man, it passes through dry places seeking rest and finds none. Then it says, 'I will return to the house I left.' And upon returning, it finds the house swept clean and put in order. Then it goes and brings seven other spirits more wicked than itself, and they enter and dwell there. And the final condition of that man is worse than the first."*

The car was already packed by the time I walked outside.

Camille stood by the driver's side, sunglasses hiding the weight in her eyes, while our daughter double-checked the dorm checklist on her phone, pretending not to notice the silence stretching between us.

Eighteen years old. Tall. Smart. Beautiful. Everything I prayed she'd be—and more. She looked back at me from the edge of adulthood with the kind of grace I'd spent my life trying to earn.

I hugged her harder than I meant to. She didn't flinch.

"I'll call when we get there," she said, her voice too calm for what this meant.

I nodded, unsure if my own voice would hold.

She turned to hug me again—this time slower, tighter.

"I'm only going to be two hours away," she said, trying to sound grown but soft around the edges.

It cracked something open in me. Not pain, but something tender. Like her voice carried all the quiet proof I needed that I had done something right.

"You saved me first," I whispered back. "You gave me a reason to stay clean. Every single day."

She pulled back just enough to look me in the eye. "You always made me feel safe, Dad. Even when you didn't feel strong."

I nodded, the lump in my throat thick as truth.

She climbed into the passenger seat. Camille gave me a knowing look—half grief, half pride—and got behind the wheel.

Then she was gone. Just like that.

I stood at the curb until the car turned the corner. Until the taillights blinked out.

And then I was alone.

The house felt bigger when I stepped back inside.

Not physically—just emptier. Like all the air had gone with her. I walked through each room like a ghost, touching things I didn't realize I'd miss. Her bedroom door still slightly open, the lingering smell of vanilla lotion and youth hanging in the air like a memory that didn't know it wasn't welcome anymore.

The silence was thick. Not peaceful. Just present.

I sat at the edge of the couch, turned the TV on, then off. Opened the fridge. Closed it. Walked to the window and stared at the street like she might come back just to grab something she forgot.

She didn't.

I wasn't used to this kind of stillness. Not after eighteen years of noise and motion and purpose. She'd been my reason to get up in the morning. To stay clean. To fight the pull of the old voice that used to whisper in the cracks of my soul.

Now that voice had room to echo.

I thought back to the night she was born—how small she looked in my hands, like she might slip through my fingers if I didn't hold her just right. I remember promising her, right there in the hospital room, that I would never let her feel the world the way it had introduced itself to me. That I'd be better for her, even if I never believed I could be better for myself.

And I was. Most days. Some days I was just

present. Others I was a shell with a steady hand. But I never slipped.

Every scraped knee, every nightlight check, every college brochure magnet on the fridge—each moment was another step away from who I used to be. She didn't just grow up under my roof. She grew up over my grave.

Now she was gone. Not gone-gone, but gone enough that the ghost I buried started pacing again.

And I didn't know what to do with the silence it left behind.

I wandered into her room again that night. Just stood in the doorway, afraid to go all the way in like stepping too far might erase what she left behind. The bed was still made, half the pillows gone. The walls looked naked where her posters had been. A stray bobby pin sat on the dresser like it didn't know it had been forgotten.

I took a step inside, slow and careful, like I was afraid to wake up the memories tucked away in this space. My fingertips brushed along the edge of her desk, pausing on the faint indentations where she'd pressed too hard with her pen while doing homework. Her handwriting was still there, etched into the wood like it had nowhere else to go. I traced the lines absently, whispering her name under my breath just to hear it in the quiet.

Her closet door hung slightly ajar, and I could see the edges of her favorite flannel shirts and the sundresses she only wore when she felt like pretending it was summer. I almost reached for one, but my hand stopped halfway, hovering in the stillness. I didn't trust myself to hold it without feeling like I'd unravel.

I sat down on her bed, the mattress giving way under my weight. It felt wrong somehow, like I was intruding. I ran my hand over the blanket, smoothing out invisible creases, remembering the nights I used to tuck her in, how she'd mumble something incoherent before rolling over and sinking back into sleep. I would stand there sometimes, just watching her breathe, counting each rise and fall of her chest like it was proof she was still here, still mine to protect.

The room still smelled faintly of her—vanilla and lavender, hints of whatever she'd been using for her hair. I closed my eyes and let it linger, let it settle in my lungs. It felt like holding my breath underwater—strange and still, the ache both sharp and familiar.

I wanted to say something, maybe whisper a prayer or an apology. But I stayed silent, letting the room speak instead. The echo of her laughter, the whisper of her voice, the way she'd hum under her breath when she thought no one was listening—it all lived here, suspended in time, untouched by the world outside.

I sat on her edge of the bed and let my hands hang between my knees, staring at the place where she used to keep her journal, her sketchpad, her favorite hoodie folded like armor. It was gone now—packed, taken. She took her things. Her laughter. Her chaos. The orbit I'd built my sobriety around.

What was I now?

I had no one to read bedtime stories to. No reason to buy another birthday cake. No fear of being found out—because the one person who needed me to stay good had already moved on believing I was.

The silence didn't just echo.

It started humming.

Low. Familiar. Like an old song trying to find its chorus.

I didn't mean to open the drawer. Didn't mean to slide the shoebox out from behind the sweaters she never wore.

But once it was in my hands, I knew what I was doing.

I carried it to the dining table like it was sacred again—like it hadn't been the reason I almost lost everything.

The scrapbook wasn't dusty. I'd been careful to keep it hidden but preserved, like a relic too dangerous to destroy.

I flipped past the dividers.

Black serial killers: Carl Eugene Watts. Chester Turner. Lorenzo Gilyard. Samuel Little. Their eyes stared back through newspaper clippings and crime scene photos.

Harrison Graham had his own page—clean, focused, meticulous. I'd underlined his court statement in red ink. *"I wanted to know what death felt like from the inside out."*

Then Gosnell—his page stained like the shame that bled through everything he ever touched.

The next section was local. Philadelphia's children of darkness: The Frankford Slasher. Antonio Rodriguez, the Kensington Strangler. Marie Noe, who killed babies with a calm face and clean sheets. Juan Edward Covington, quiet and cruel.

And tucked in the back—The Messenger.

Clippings. Photos. Notes. Not all of it from public record. Not all of it easy to look at.

The book didn't hum like the silence did.

It breathed.

Each page was a ritual. Each face a sermon.

I told myself I kept the scrapbook for research. To understand what made a man cross the line from want to need. To study how they got caught—or didn't. But the truth was simpler, and darker: it made me feel seen. Like some piece of me—

sharp-edged and sleepless—had ancestors.

I had catalogued them for years. On the surface, it was just paper and ink. But underneath, it was memory, compulsion, prophecy.

Eighteen years of control, of walking the narrow path, of waking up and choosing the right thing over the real thing.

I stayed clean. Every day. Every hour. Even on the nights when I couldn't sleep, and the air got heavy with old music. Even when Camille would look at me sideways, sensing something she couldn't name. Even when the Messenger roared in the back of my skull like a caged choir.

I stayed clean. For her.

But now she was gone. And with her went the structure—the breath-by-breath rhythm of being needed.

Discipline without direction is just hunger with manners. And I had fed myself well on fatherhood.

But now the house was quiet. My hands were still. The shadows no longer feared being seen.

What did a man do with all the tools of self-control when the one reason he wielded them had packed up and moved two hours away?

I didn't know.

So I sat in the quiet, stared at the scrapbook, and waited to hear what the silence wanted to teach me next.

It didn't whisper. It didn't scream.

It crept.

Like water finding the weakest part of the foundation. Like heat rising through old floorboards. Like memory—that first addiction.

The silence held out its hands and offered me a mirror. Not the man I was, or the father I had become—but the ache beneath all of it. The shadow that never truly left, only learned how to wait.

Eighteen years I held it back with bedtime stories, school drop-offs, and Sunday pancakes. I masked it with dance recitals and college visits. Built fences out of love and hope and the soft weight of a child sleeping against my chest.

But fences decompose. And shadows climb.

And when there's no one left to protect, a man starts to wonder what he's protecting himself from.

The truth is: I didn't miss the act. I missed the clarity. The stillness of decision. The focus that came with knowing who I was, even if that person terrified me.

And in that moment, with the scrapbook open and the silence blooming like mold in my lungs— I wasn't afraid.

I was curious.

Curiosity didn't feel like a flame—it felt like a pulse. Steady. Measured. Patient.

I didn't leap back into blood. I circled it. I observed it the way a surgeon watches a wound before he makes the first cut.

The science of death had changed since I last let it in. Forensics wasn't just technique—it was theology. A new doctrine. And I became a student with reverence.

I knew about Luminol and touch DNA, trace evidence and shoeprint patterns. I learned how fibers cling to car seats and how cellphone towers betray your location even when you swear you were somewhere else.

There were whole podcasts dedicated to mistakes—slipups that cracked cases open years after the last scream. Reddit threads, court documents, FBI case files. I devoured them.

And the more I read, the more I realized just how many people had gotten lazy.

Arrogant.

The world had grown loud and clumsy. Cameras were everywhere, sure—but so was distraction. Everyone thought they were watching, but no one really paid attention. Even justice got bored if it couldn't scroll.

But I didn't scroll. I studied.

Every podcast became scripture. Every unsolved thread a hymn. Every cracked case a sermon I dissected line by line.

I would listen in the dark, the glow of my laptop screen painting my face in pale blue as whispers of cold cases drifted through my headphones. My hands would hover over the keyboard, fingers pressing play, pause, rewind, scribbling notes in the margins of my old journals—scripture numbers, dates, locations. The language of their violence became familiar, almost poetic.

It wasn't about fascination. It was about absolution. About control.
I had spent years clawing my way back to the surface, dragging pieces of myself out of the mud, scraping off the residue of my past. I was the man who chose the narrow path, who stitched together a life from shredded faith and borrowed grace. But the deeper I went into their stories, the more I saw my own reflection stitched between the lines.

They were whispers of what I had buried. Of what I had strangled beneath layers of routine and redemption. They lived where I once did—on the edge of impulse and intention, a cliff I teetered over and nearly plummeted from. Their stories were my ghost stories, echoes of decisions I almost made, sins I almost committed. But the truth?

I had made those decisions.

I had committed those sins.

I cataloged them with precision—colored tabs, timestamps, cross-referenced with local newspapers and police bulletins. Red for bloodless disappearances. Blue for public executions. Yellow for bodies found posed like confessions. I traced their paths like scripture, connecting dots on city maps with red thread, the lines stretching across intersections and side streets like veins. I studied the geography of violence, the rhythm of death, the pulsing beat of cities that fed on their own forgotten.

But it wasn't just curiosity. It wasn't just a morbid fascination.

It was penance.

I told myself it was study—an academic exercise to understand the minds that fell into the abyss. But I wasn't trying to understand them. I was trying to understand me.

I had walked away from that life. I had turned my back on the hunger, forced it into submission, chained it beneath the weight of routine and fatherhood. But it wasn't gone. It just went quiet, like an animal learning to hide.

Every late night spent listening to those stories, every page of the scrapbook I leafed through in the quiet hours when the house slept—it wasn't research.

It was communion.

It was confession.

A ritual to remember what I had done and what I had given up to be who I was now.

Because this time, I wasn't chasing chaos. I was composing something sacred, something sharp. A symphony of silence and precision.

The language of their crimes began to feel like a song I was learning to play by ear—each note ringing out clearer, each verse sung louder in the stillness of my mind. I started to understand the rhythm of it, the spaces where hesitation lived, where mistakes bled through the seams. I knew where they faltered. I saw where they hesitated. Where they gave in to impulse instead of discipline.

The ones who failed were sloppy, careless. I watched their arrogance lead them to ruin. I studied documentaries of them getting caught: hands cuffed behind their backs, eyes wide with disbelief, like they had never considered that their story might end in a cage. I would pause the footage, lean closer to the screen, and study their faces. I wasn't looking for fear. I was looking for where they broke.

Because that was the part I couldn't forget. I knew what it was to break. To snap beneath the weight of hunger and rage. To reach for redemption but find only dirt beneath my nails and blood beneath my skin. I had walked away from that edge. I had forced myself back from the brink. But the hunger was still there, whispering beneath my skin like an unspoken prayer.

I wasn't going back. I was going forward—into something darker, yes. But cleaner. Sharper. Holy in its intention.

It wasn't just about control. It was about redemption. I had to know if I could do it differently. If the darkness that lived inside me could be refined, sharpened into something that wasn't just chaos but purpose.
I began to catalog new rituals. Early morning

runs through the city—mapping routes, memorizing alleys that twisted away from main streets, watching where shadows lingered longest. I noted where the streetlights blinked out, where security cameras were more for show than protection. I timed my walks, learning the rhythm of each block, the habits of the people who passed through it.

I bought a burner phone. An unmarked notebook with smooth, thick pages that wouldn't bleed through. I filled it with scripture—not just from the Bible, but from the old texts I found online: Dante, Milton, even fragments of Hindu and Buddhist teachings that spoke of cleansing, rebirth, the purging of sin. I wrote them with care, the ink smooth and deliberate, like I was etching them into stone. I began to memorize them. I whispered them under my breath as I walked through the city, reciting them like prayers.

I wasn't in a rush. That's where they went wrong—the others. They lunged at the impulse, clawed at the first opportunity like animals starving for a kill. But I was patient. I let the ache build, stretching it taut until it thrummed in my bones. I fed it with knowledge, sharpened it with study. Every night, I read the scriptures I had written, my fingers brushing over the pages like rosary beads. I spoke them to the silence, let the words fill the hollow places. I let them replace the cravings that once plagued me.

And yet, even with all the study, all the careful preparation, I felt urgency stirring beneath the calm.

Not desperation—necessity.

Because knowing wasn't enough. Reading, cataloguing, dissecting—it kept the beast fed, but not full. My ache didn't want information. It wanted incarnation.

Addiction never leaves. It waits.

The world teaches you to speak about it like it's something you've beaten, something you've conquered with the right meetings and enough time. They give you chips, small tokens that mark your progress, like you've crossed borders and burned the maps behind you. But the truth?

Addiction is a squatter.

It sets up residence in the hollow places of your bones. You evict it a thousand times, but it leaves things behind: memories, impulses, whispers that linger like dust in the corners. You paint over the cracks, nail the windows shut, but it slips back in with the cold air, threading itself into your breath when you're not paying attention.

People say one day at a time like it's a prayer, but really, it's a warning. Because every morning is a new fight to keep the door closed, to sweep the glass from the threshold, to ignore the knock that comes soft and steady just behind your eyes.

I had replaced one addiction with another. Instead of needles, it was scriptures. Instead of cracked vials, it was newspaper clippings and police reports.

And the idea of not fighting... that was more terrifying than anything.

Because I knew what waited on the other side of surrender.

I knew the taste of it.

I knew what it meant to give in.

And I was afraid of what might happen if I waited too long. Afraid the precision I'd built would dull. Afraid that the discipline I'd mastered would curdle into rot, and the next time I acted, it wouldn't be clean—it would be clumsy. Emotional.

I didn't want bloodlust.

I wanted control.

And to hold it, I had to use it.

But I didn't rush. Eighteen years had taught me patience.

So I listened.

Not with my ears, but with the part of me that had been waiting in the quiet—the part that knew how to read shadows and silences. I let the city unfold itself, street by street, like a scripture I hadn't prayed through in years.

I didn't go out hunting. I drifted.

Long walks after dark. A different route home. A coffee shop seat that let me see the front and back doors at once. I watched how people moved when they thought no one noticed. I watched how the city breathed when it exhaled the people it didn't care to protect.

And eventually, I saw her. Not a target. Not yet. Just a woman carved from routine and neglect. The kind who walked like her story wasn't being written anymore—just repeated.

She passed me three nights in a row. Same coat. Same steps. Same sag in her shoulders like something in her had long since caved in.

I didn't follow her that night.

I waited.

Camille wanted to help our daughter settle in, walk the campus again, see where the next chapter would unfold.

I told her to take her time.

She didn't know I meant it differently.

The house had been mine alone for five days.

And silence makes its move best when no one else is listening.

Because after eighteen years of silence, I knew better than to light the first spark.

But on the fourth night, the air felt different. The silence shifted. And I got up.

Slow. Deliberate. Hungry—but precise.

I stayed half a block behind her.

Close enough to track her rhythm, far enough not to disturb it. She turned left on Allegheny, then crossed past an old laundromat where half the neon letters had burned out. She didn't look back. Most people don't. Not when the world has taught them that danger wears a mask they already know.

She moved like she was heading nowhere, which meant she probably didn't expect to be followed home.

Except I didn't follow her home.

I followed her to the place she stopped. A chain-link fence. An alley I'd mapped days earlier. No cameras. No light. The kind of space the city forgets until someone bleeds in it.

I stood still and let the night press its weight against my skin.

I hadn't brought a weapon. I didn't need one.

When the moment came, it wouldn't be about rage. It would be about execution.

Clean. Fast. Unseen.

And I was ready to begin.

She paused near a dumpster at the edge of the alley, tugging at her coat collar like it might protect her from more than the cold.

I stepped closer.

Each footfall measured. Soft. Intentional.

She didn't hear me. Or if she did, she didn't believe I was a threat. That's how most people die—not in fear, but in disbelief.

I reached for her—not violently. Not with chaos. Just a hand on her shoulder, steady as scripture.

She turned.

There was no scream. Just a widening of the eyes. A flicker of recognition, not of who I was, but of what I had come to do.

My other hand moved quick—precise. The pressure was practiced. Calculated. She didn't fall hard. Didn't fight long.

It was over before the night finished exhaling.

I didn't need to look back. Her stillness was confirmation enough.

No panic. No euphoria. Just the slow returning of breath and awareness—like waking from a dream I hadn't realized I was dreaming.

I walked home with calm hands and a steady heart.

The silence was different now. Not empty but listening. Waiting.

I stood up from the table, ready to shower off the night, when something tugged at me.

Not a thought. Not a feeling.

A snag—sharp and sudden, just above the ankle.

It had happened earlier—just after the alley, when I slipped through the gate. I felt it then, low and near my ankle. Barely noticeable. Just a catch. Something I forgot as quickly as it happened.

But now, as I pulled off my sock, I saw it.

A faint smear of blood. Dried, dark, clinging to the inside like it had been waiting.

I checked for a wound—my shoe, the hem of my pants, the skin above my ankle. Nothing. No tear. No pain. No memory of how it got there.

Just proof.

The kind of mistake that doesn't scream.

It whispers.

You weren't as careful as you thought.

My heart didn't race. It narrowed.

It wasn't the blood that shook me.

It was the unknown.

I dropped my coat at the door and made my way to the bathroom. The lights stayed off. I didn't need reflection to know what I'd done. But curiosity lingered.

So, I let the blade rest against my skin.

Not to bleed. Not to escape.

Just to feel the edge.

The cold was sobering. Not sharp enough to cut, but precise enough to remind me how close I stood to the line.

In that still moment, I understood I wouldn't be able to stop this. Not again. And if I couldn't control the next descent, the only mercy left was to silence the voice before it found someone else.

I hadn't just reopened a door.

I'd invited something in.

And it would not be leaving.

Back at the table, I stared at the scrapbook. Not as a collector. Not as a student.

But as the final author in a gospel written in blood.

And if I loved Camille—if I truly loved our daughter—I knew this couldn't continue in the light.

They couldn't witness the rot returning. Couldn't be collateral to my curiosity.

I wasn't ready to write the end.

But I had begun to sense it.

Something else was watching from the corners of my mind—still patient, but closer than ever.

And if I couldn't stop what was coming...

...I could at least get out of its way.

I am to vanish, let it not be in fear— but in fire.

So that the silence may be inherited by something stronger than I could ever be.

So I gathered what I could—not a confession, but a reckoning. Not for forgiveness, but for inheritance. I left it all in the scrapbook—the scriptures of silence, the psalms of murder, the hymns of memory inked in clipped headlines and blood-slick truths. These pages are not for me. They are for the one who will someday read them and understand that monsters are not born in the dark, but molded in the light—shaped by silence, fed by fear.

If this gospel must continue, let it be read with understanding and an awakened soul.

Let the ink dry in blood—so when he turns these pages, he feels the weight of it all: the guilt, the hunger, a curse inked in scripture and carved into flesh.

And if I am the house—swept, emptied, and waiting—then what returns next may be more wicked than even I dared to become.

I leave not only my truths, but my goodbyes— letters folded between scripture and shadow, waiting to be unearthed when the silence finally.

THOU SHALT NOT BURY THE TRUTH

I wasn't supposed to live this long. Not with the things I've done. Not with the weight I carry. Yet here I am, pen pressed to paper, trying to spill the rot from my soul the only way I know how—with words. They were always my salvation, my grandfather's gift, and my curse. He used to say that words were the closest thing we had to immortality. That if I wrote something true enough, it would outlive me. But I'm not looking for immortality. I'm looking for absolution.

There's a scripture that echoes in my head, one I've tried to drown out but always returns—like it's tethered to my marrow. *"For nothing is hidden that will not be made manifest, nor is anything secret that will not be known and come to light."* I wonder sometimes if that's what this is. If writing it down is the only way to bring it to light. To make sense of it. To bleed it out before it consumes me whole.

This isn't a confession—not in the way you might think. I'm not asking for forgiveness. I don't expect redemption. I've seen too much to believe in that anymore. But I do believe in the power of truth. I believe that some stories aren't meant to be buried. That some darkness, no matter how deep, needs to be spoken aloud.

They called me many things: a monster, a phantom, a ghost in the alleys where good men dared not tread. They painted me in shades of evil, their headlines screaming for justice they never found. But they didn't know me. They never saw the why. They only saw the what.

I have learned that survival is a scripture in itself, one written not in words but in the desperate acts of those clinging to the edge. I have etched mine in flesh and fear, a gospel for the forgotten. They say redemption is a path you walk, but for me, it's a wound that never closes.

This is my reckoning. My scripture written in blood and memory. If you've made it this far, you're here to witness—not to judge. You're searching for meaning. Looking for the why. Maybe you want to understand me. Or maybe you just want to watch me burn. But I don't need your mercy.

I don't even want it.

I just need you to understand. To see what I saw. To know that every act, every moment, was part of something greater than myself.

It doesn't matter. You are here, and that is enough. If you want answers, if you want to peer into the depths of this shadow, then read on. But I warn you—what you're looking for isn't buried.

It's festering just beneath the surface, raw and seeping, waiting to be seen.

I have written it all. Every drop of blood. Every sin. Every letter.

It begins now.

I've carried these memories like stones in my pockets, dragging them from one shadow to the next. They've grown heavier with each passing year, sinking me further into the dark. Tonight, I choose to let them go.

As I glance at the bottle on the table, the white pills stacked neatly inside like tiny promises. Salvation in chemical form. The label is smudged, worn from months of turning it over in my hands, always lingering on the edge of decision.

Tonight is different. Tonight, I'm ready to let it all go. Not out of fear. Not out of regret. But because the story is told. The ink is dry. There is nothing left to say.

I twist the cap, listen to the soft rattle as they spill into my palm. I wonder if they will be enough. I hope they will be enough.

I raise the glass of water to my lips, the chill biting my tongue. I pause, just for a moment, staring at the words on the page one last time. My gospel. My truth. My reckoning.

The pills taste bitter as they slide down, but the water is smooth, washing them away like they were never there at all.

And then, I wait.

The letters are done. The words are written. The story has been told. And I am ready to close the book.

It ends here.

My name is Derrick. And this was my gospel.

To my wife and my daughter,

If you're reading this, it means I've run out of time—or I chose to stop running.
I don't expect forgiveness, and I'm not writing to beg for it. I'm writing because silence would be a greater sin than anything I've already done. You deserve more than rumors, headlines, or the fragments someone else might try to piece together. You deserve the truth—from me, and only me.

There's a story behind the man I became. A truth buried beneath years of sobriety, fatherhood, Sunday dinners, and quiet mornings where I pretended the past couldn't touch me. But it did. It always did. I lived two lives.

One you knew—the man who tucked you in, who grilled on weekends, who held your hand at the doctor's office and rubbed your back during sleepless nights.

And another you didn't—the man who carried ghosts in his blood, who atoned with actions but never confessions. Until now.

This isn't a goodbye. It's a reckoning in ink. I spent today compiling the pieces of me I never dared to share—notes from my journals, poems I scrawled in the margins of old newspapers, and memories too heavy for ordinary conversation. Each word was written with trembling hands, each sentence a step toward surrender. What's unveiled in these pages is the truth I've hidden and the legacy I hope to leave behind. I'm terrified you'll see me differently once you know everything, but it would be a greater cruelty to leave you in the dark. And so I write, because I cannot run anymore.

I want you both to know that I tried. I tried harder than I ever thought I could—to be good, to be clean, to be the man you both deserved. But some ghosts don't fade; they just learn to whisper. And I spent years listening to them. Pretending I didn't. Hiding behind redemption like it could somehow hold back the tide. But it was always there—scratching at the edges, whispering through the cracks.

I loved you both with everything I had, even the broken parts. Especially the broken parts. I wanted so badly to be enough—to outrun my own shadow, to hold you both so tightly that the dark couldn't slip between us. I wanted to build walls high enough that nothing could get in. But I realize now that I was only ever walling myself in. And I'm sorry for that.

You were my redemption. Every laugh, every shared glance, every moment I got to be your husband and your father was a reprieve I never earned. I don't deserve the memories I carry of you both—like snapshots I hoarded in the corners of my mind, pulling them out when the whispers grew too loud.

Your laughter was my armor. Your love, my lifeline. And I held onto it with shaking hands, afraid that if I ever loosened my grip, I would drown.

I tried to make peace with my past, but peace is a language I never learned to speak. And now, as the walls close in, I realize that redemption is not something you hold. It's something you pass on. And that's where David's son comes in.

David L. Powell III. A name I wouldn't learn until much later. But the first time I saw him, I knew.

He couldn't have been more than sixteen, stocking shelves at a pharmacy under the washed-out glow of the store's essence. I remember watching him from the end of the aisle, the way he moved—steady, deliberate, careful. It was like looking back in time, staring straight into the reflection of a ghost.

His shoulders had that same squared determination, the way David used to stand when he was bracing himself for bad news. The way his brow furrowed when he counted bottles, lips pressed into that familiar line of focus—I'd seen it before. Years ago. A thousand times.

I stepped back into the shadow of the aisle, my pulse thrumming in my ears. I told myself it wasn't possible. But then he turned, just for a moment, and the light hit his face in a way that made my breath catch. The same sharp jawline. The same intensity simmering behind his eyes. David's eyes.

I almost called out. Almost let his name slip past my lips like a prayer I hadn't meant to whisper. But I didn't. I just watched. Watched him work. Watched him move. Watched the echoes of a man I'd buried years ago walk the earth again in the bones of his son.

I didn't speak. Not then. I wasn't ready to unravel that thread, to test the strength of it. But I knew. I knew blood when I saw it.

For years, I tried to find David. You remember the name from the stories I told, the only friend I ever truly had before the streets swallowed us both. He was a lifeline during my darkest years— but by the time I had the strength to look, he was gone. Vanished. No trace. It felt like failing all over again.

But the universe wasn't finished with me. It had given me another chance—a chance to make things right. And I wasn't going to let it slip through my fingers.

Years later, I came across a manuscript—a raw, unflinching look at pain, history, and survival. The name on the cover stopped my breath. It was his. I reached out under the pretense of editing, and we started talking. I told myself it was mentorship, but the truth is, I needed to see if that light had lasted.
It had.

Let him have these pages. That is my most sacred request. Let him carry them forward, let him decide when the world is ready. Let him be the keeper of this truth, not to glorify me, but to show that even monsters may be born from pain, and even murderers might once have been sons, friends, fathers.

And if I failed you both, then let this be my penance. Let my confessions breathe outside the walls I built to contain them. Let David's son decide what happens next.

Know this: you were my redemption. In every laugh, every kiss goodnight, every morning you woke me up with sleepy eyes and tangled hair—I found pieces of the man I wished I could have been. For you, I tried. I swear I tried.

I love you both more than I ever found words to say. But words are all I have left now. And I hope they are enough to tell you that you were my light in a world that was always too dark.

If I'm gone now, it's not because I wanted to leave you.

It's because I couldn't outrun what I was.

I hope one day, you'll understand.

I hope one day, you'll find it in your hearts to forgive me.

Forgive me, if you can. Remember me, if you must.
And know that in the end, I chose to stop running.

I have written **Ten Requests** within the pages that follow. They are not commandments, nor are they demands. They are the last wishes of a man who wants to leave behind something more than shadows and whispers. They are my penance, my final offering.

My Ten Final Requests

1. **Bury me quietly.**
   No fanfare. No ministers paid to lie on my behalf. Just you, and maybe her, if she wants to come. Find that plot we looked at years ago, the one by the tree where you said the sun would hit just right in spring. Wrap me in something plain. No suit. Just something soft. Let me return to the dirt the way I came into this world—unadorned.

2. **Visit the place where we first danced.**
   Remember how you laughed when I stepped on your toes, then kissed me anyway? That place still echoes with that memory. Go back there. Take her if she'll go. Let her see where love started. Play the same song. Let her see joy didn't begin with her, but she became its center.

3. **Forgive only if it frees you.**
   Don't force yourself to speak well of me. Don't carry guilt if you feel anger. If forgiveness breaks a chain, then let it break. But if it binds you tighter, let it go. Either way, do it for you—not for me.

4. **Tell our daughter who I really was.**
   Not just the man who danced in the

kitchen or made pancakes in silly shapes. Tell her I was broken. That I hurt people. That I tried to build something beautiful on the ruins of my past. Let her choose what to remember, but let her remember *all* of me.

5. **Keep the music alive.**
   Dust off the record player. Play Nina, Donny, and Marvin. Dance in the living room when no one's watching. Let her feel the weight and warmth of those sounds. Let her know they weren't just songs — they were survival.

6. **Don't let her carry my shame.**
   My name shouldn't be her burden. Let it be her banner. Show her she can be better than me — *that she already is*. Let her craft a story with her own hands, not inherit mine like a scar.

7. **Read the Psalms I marked.**
   I found myself in the verses. In the desperation. In the cries for mercy. They were the only prayers I ever truly believed. When I was too ashamed to kneel, I read. When I was too weak to speak, I whispered them. Maybe they'll speak to you too.

8. **Burn the clothes from that night.**
   They're in the crawlspace, wrapped in that blue tarp. You'll know them by the weight of what they've seen. Don't try to wash them. Don't try to explain them. Let fire do what I never could—destroy the evidence of what I became.

9. **Say my name without lowering your voice.**
   Don't let neighbors, news anchors, or officers define me. Speak my name in the open. Say it loud when you tell her about the good days. Say it soft when you talk about the hard ones. But *say it*. Let my memory exist in truth.

10. **Give this manuscript to David L. Powell III.**
    Wrap it in the leather folder on my desk. Include this letter. He'll know what it means. Ask him to wait ten years. Let the dust settle. Let hearts heal. Then tell him to tell it *all*. Tell him to paint me exactly as I was. Let him be the voice I never had the courage to use.

Now comes the hardest part.

Goodbye.

You gave me a chance to be whole. Even if I never truly was. You let me taste normalcy, fatherhood, laughter. You gave me the world I never thought I could deserve.

And I gave you a haunted man who tried like hell to be better.

By the time you read this, I may already be gone. By choice or consequence—I'm not sure which found me first. But I know the truth will follow me either way.

I don't know what the headlines will say, or what the law will find. I only know what I leave behind:

Love. Regret. Truth.

And you.

Always you.

—*D.*

Dear David L. Powell III,

You don't know me, and I don't know what you'll think of this. I'm not writing this to make sense of it all. I'm still trying to make sense of it myself. What he left behind wasn't just a story—it was pain. Something I didn't know he was still carrying. Something I'm not sure I'll ever fully understand.

I didn't see it. Or maybe I just didn't want to. I remember waking up some nights, reaching out for him, only to find his side of the bed empty. The sheets were cold. The room felt bigger. He was just gone. I would lie there, staring at the ceiling, wondering where he went. What could pull him from our bed in the middle of the night? I never asked. I guess I was afraid of what he'd say. Maybe I just didn't want to know.

I should have read the signs. The long nights. The restless pacing. The way his eyes would sometimes look right through me, like I wasn't even there. I told myself it was just stress. Work. The pressure of everything we were building. But now I know it was more. It was always more.

There were nights I'd hear him in his office, talking to himself, the pen scratching against the paper for hours. I would stand at the door sometimes, my hand on the knob, but I never went in. I didn't want to break whatever silence he had found. I didn't want him to stop. I don't know why. I should have asked. I should have opened the door. I didn't.

He talked about you. More than I realized. He said you reminded him of someone he lost. He said your writing had something in it, something he couldn't describe. I didn't understand it then. I do now.

I read everything. His journals. His letters. Every word. I cried. I cursed him. I laughed once or twice. I wanted to tear it all up and burn it. But I didn't. Because I think he meant it. I think he wanted you to see him, really see him, even if no one else could.

He asked me to give this to you. So here it is. His journals. His letters. His truth. His final act.

He told me to wait ten years. He said you would need that time. That you would need to grieve. To understand. He said you'd know when it was time. Just don't let it die in a drawer. Don't let him vanish into a headline or some whispered rumor.

I don't know if this is closure or if it's just tearing the wound open again. Maybe it's both. I loved him. I still do. Even with everything I know now. Even with the weight of it. I still love him. Maybe that makes me weak. Maybe that makes me something worse. But it's the truth.

I wish I could have saved him. I wish I had opened that door. I wish I had asked the right questions. I wish I had been braver. I wish I had loved him better. I wish I had seen him, really seen him, before it was too late.

Tell it how it happened. Tell it like it hurt. Like it mattered. Just… tell it.

—His wife

From the Desk of David L. Powell III

There are some moments that ask you to become more than you were the day before. When I opened that box, I stepped into one.

It wasn't about curiosity. It wasn't even about courage. It was about obligation—something deeper than duty. A calling, maybe. A weight passed from one life to another with the hope it wouldn't be dropped.

What Derrick left behind wasn't just a series of memories etched out on paper—it was marrow. His words weren't written in ink. They bled. Through grief. Through memory. Through the cracks of a life lived in conflict.

He didn't come to me seeking praise. He came seeking truth. And that truth, however brutal, deserved to breathe.

He asked me to wait ten years. I did. Stories like this one need time to settle—like dust in a room that's finally gone quiet. And now, in that stillness, I open the window and let the world in.

Because some truths demand daylight. Because silence is a kind of burial. Because he believed someone had to remember him whole.

And somehow, that someone became me.

Reading Derrick's words felt like walking into a house I'd only seen from the outside. Every room was familiar and foreign. Every sentence felt like stepping onto a floor that hadn't been walked in years—soft with dust, loud with memory, unsure if it would hold. I kept hearing his voice in my head, low and deliberate, like he was reading over my shoulder.

He wrote the way I try to write—like memory matters. Like every detail, every scar, every flicker of light deserves to be seen.

There was something else I noticed when I read his words. Sometimes, his reflection on the past would change, almost like he was slipping back into those moments, living them again in real time. It wasn't just memory. It was reliving. His writing would shift—his sentences sharper, his descriptions clearer, the lines between then and now blurring until you couldn't tell if you were reading a memory or witnessing it unfold. I think he needed that. To not just remember, but to live it again. To feel it. To bleed it out one more time.

His wife's letter sat on top, shaking in its simplicity. I read it three times. Not because I didn't understand it, but because I wanted to feel what she felt. Anger. Loss. A strange kind of loyalty that only love—or trauma—can forge.

I never expected to be the one holding the story. I was just a kid writing poems about my city, trying to capture something real. But Derrick saw something in me. At first, it was just conversations—small talks about writing, about pain, about survival. He'd give me books, tell me to read them, then ask what I thought. Over time, those conversations grew deeper, stretched longer. He shared pieces of himself bit by bit, as if testing whether I could handle the weight of it. Eventually, it became something more. Not just mentorship, but a friendship built on unspoken truths and shadows we both carried. Now, I understand our connection. Why he finally let me in. He was preparing me for this.

He didn't want this to be forgotten. He didn't want to be remembered only as a shadow, or as the name whispered across newsrooms and headlines—The Messenger—a title he never owned, never enough to define the man beneath.

So here I am, ten years later. Telling it.

Telling all of it.

Not to justify him. Not to save him. But to say: this happened. This man lived. This man hurt. This man tried.

And if there's any redemption in this story, it's not in the killing or the confessions.

It's in the fact that he trusted someone else to carry the truth.

That someone was me.

I have changed the names of some and omitted certain details to protect those still living. Derrick was never caught for his crimes, and what you hold now is the truth that only I know. The truth that he trusted me to tell.

I carry this story not out of obligation, but out of love. Because what Derrick gave me wasn't just a glimpse into his world. He gave me purpose. He saw something in me that I couldn't see in myself.

He handed me the weight of his truth and trusted me not to break under it.

I promised him I wouldn't.

This is for him. This is for the truth.

—David L. Powell III

ABOUT THE AUTHOR

David L. Powell III is an author, screenwriter, and storyteller known for his gripping narratives and deep exploration of the human condition. With a strong background in ghostwriting and over 20 scripts to his name, David brings a unique voice to his work, blending real-life unsolved cases with fictionalized accounts to explore themes of redemption, moral struggle, and the complexities of the human psyche.

David's personal connection to the narratives he creates allows him to bring an authenticity and depth to his characters, who are as complex as the stories they inhabit. *Blood & Scriptures: Memoirs of the Philadelphia Slasher* immerses readers in a raw, intense perspective on crime and identity, drawing from his own life experiences and the intricate web of human relationships.

An advocate for empowerment, David's work resonates with those who understand the complexities of life, human frailty, and the pursuit of justice. He lives in Pennsylvania, where he continues to write and develop new projects that challenge both himself and his readers.

www.ingramcontent.com/pod-product-compliance
Lightning Source LLC
Chambersburg PA
CBHW070315310726
48976CB00005B/1718